MONSTERS AND MACHINES

A STRANGE HAPPENINGS COLLECTION

KELSEY JOSEPHSON

Monsters and Machines is a collection of the first five Strange Happenings short stories. These tales follow the adventures of Rosie and Lucille at the 1893 Chicago World's Fair in an alternate universe, where steampunk technology clashes with the monstrous.

SOMETHING HAPPENED ON THE WAY TO THE WORLD'S FAIR

The firebox flames danced on Rosie Weston's skin, highlighting white and bronze vitiligo as she shoveled in one last load of coal. The steam engine was hungry, demanding more fuel in the pelting rain. Rosie hung the shovel by the coal pile and stretched her burning muscles.

"That should do until the last stretch to Chicago."

Engineer Honora Quaman grunted in response, eyes fixed on the locomotive's gauges. To Rosie's dismay, the wiry crone kept to herself more often than not during their late-night shifts.

Undaunted, Rosie tried again. "Are you staying for the Fair?"

"No. Too much work to do."

Rosie settled in her rear-facing window seat and fished her leather logbook out from under the chair. A colorful flyer for the World's Fair served as a bookmark. It highlighted details for a spectacular opening ceremony and demonstrations from Nikola Tesla. She turned to the marked page and sketched schematics for the coal-shoveling device she was building in her head.

"Are you writing in your diary again?"

"It's a logbook!"

Honora snorted. "Whatever you say."

Rosie was deep into her sketch when a yellow lantern signaled in her peripheral vision. Belatedly, she realized all the passenger cars were dark. Even during the night, a few should have been lit for safety.

Rosie jumped up, knocking her logbook to the floor. Grateful her coal-stained cheeks hid her blush, she stashed it in the back pocket of her coveralls. "Patrick's signaling me. It's the lights again. Are you set here?"

"I've got this." Honora turned to Rosie, scowling. "Those damn lights are more trouble than they're worth. Passengers are too pampered these days. Electric lights for overnight trains. Ridiculous."

"Careful, or you'll be starting your stories with 'back in my day.' Don't you like being able to see? It could be so much worse. Remember the belt system?" Rosie shuddered. "It was so unreliable."

Honora rolled her eyes. She went back to the front of the cab. "Don't forget your tools and come back quickly. There's a sharp turn in 45. I'll need extra eyes."

"I forgot once." Rosie muttered, but she double-checked her tool belt before jotting down the time in her logbook. 1:16 am.

Outside, Rosie scaled the tender with ease, mindful of her kerosene lantern. A few years as brakeman gave her all the practice she needed to fearlessly scramble over moving trains in any weather. Still, she envied Honora, who was warm and dry in the cab.

By the time Rosie was in the darkened baggage car, she was soaked. A third of the car served as the mechanical room, while the rest stored luggage and the railway workers' personal effects. She grabbed a towel from her locker and dried off as best as she could. The coal dust combined with rain left the towel patterned light and dark like her skin.

Moving to the mechanical side, Rosie quickly spotted a loose terminal on the transformer. She turned off the huge circuit breaker and set about tightening the terminal by the lamplight. With another throw of the breaker switch, the Tesla coil crackled to life. White-blue electricity sparked around the machine, bathing everything in the car with an eerie glow. The light bulbs on the cargo side of the car lit up. Rosie smiled, satisfied with her work.

A thud sounded over the humming Tesla coil, making Rosie jump. She hopped over the low barrier separating the cargo from the generator. It was normal for trunks to shift as the train barreled down the tracks. Because of the fair, the cargo this trip was markedly different from usual. Machines and gadgets were carefully wedged between stacks of steamer trunks. She wondered if she'd get to see any of the equipment demonstrated at the Exposition.

A lone trunk stuck out at an odd angle from the rows of cargo, and a chain coiled around its middle. The large padlock in the center piqued Rosie's curiosity. She crept towards the trunk. Was it always this crooked? Aside from the heavy chain, the trunk looked no different from any of the others stuffed in the baggage car.

Rosie kneeled next to the trunk. Careful not to touch the pristine lid with her coal-stained hands, she pressed her ear against the strange luggage. She shrunk back immediately, shivering. The trunk was freezing. She leaned forward to inspect it when an abrupt knock on the door closest to the passenger cars made her jump a second time. She scurried away from the cargo.

Rosie slid the door open a fraction of an inch. Outside, the wind whipped around the train.

A woman wearing a burgundy cloak stood at the door, fist poised to knock again. Thin wire spectacles slid down her beaky nose. The howling wind tried but couldn't drown her voice entirely. "I know passengers aren't permitted in the baggage car, but I'm worried about my equipment. It's delicate. Please let me in."

Rosie hesitated.

Thunder cracked outside.

"Please, it'll only take a moment. I'll be ruined if it's damaged."

Rosie stepped back and slid the door open. "Be quick about it."

Honora would be furious if she knew.

"Why are you up so late?" Rosie blurted as the stranger entered the car.

The woman looked frantically around the room, clicking her tongue as at the instruments and equipment pushed to the side. "I never sleep well. The power flickering made me concerned for my cargo. I can see my fears were not entirely misplaced." She pulled her cloak's hood down, revealing brunette hair with a streak of white pulled into a severe bun. Her pale face was ageless.

Rosie flushed. Loading cargo wasn't her job, but she felt defensive for her fellow workers. "I'm sure they did the best they could. It's normal for vibrations to shift cargo."

The stranger's gaze fell to the chain-wrapped trunk. She rushed over to it and examined the padlock. The woman looked up at Rosie. "Has anyone disturbed this trunk?"

Rosie shifted her weight. Tension between her shoulders throbbed. She should get back to the engine. "I moved it back. It shifted with the other luggage."

The woman pursed her lips. "That's reasonable." She checked the chain again, pulling it tight.

"If you don't mind me asking, what is it?"

The stranger straightened. "It's my life's work. The culmination of years of biochemical engineering research. It's not perfect. Not yet. If my grant proposal had been accepted, I would have had the funding to make it so, but alas. We could have the future now, but society clings to fear." The woman shook her head and gave Rosie a sad smile. "No matter. My work is ready to be presented at the fair. If all goes well, it'll revolutionize the field."

"I see." Rosie wasn't sure if she understood, but this was the most anyone had talked to her in days.

"You don't, of course, but thank you." The stranger turned around, facing the trunk again. "If you'll excuse me, I must check my equipment."

"Wait, what's your name?" At the woman's inquisitive glance, she added, "It's for my records."

The woman sniffed. "Dr. Zona Prendergast."

"Thank you," Rosie replied, feeling foolish. She flipped her logbook past her sketches to a blank page and jotted Dr. Prendergast's name down while the doctor watched. "I'm Rosie Weston if you need anything. I'd shake your hand, but mine are in terrible shape." She held up her blackened hands sheepishly.

"Yes. Perhaps that would be best." Dr. Prendergast turned her attention back to her equipment.

Silence stretched awkwardly. Dr. Prendergast didn't seem to remember Rosie was there. She watched as the doctor moved from machine to machine, carefully checking over every detail.

"You said biochemical engineering?" The words came out in a rush. Rosie held her breath.

"I did." The doctor turned around, thin eyebrows raised.

"Does that mean you do medical research?"

Dr. Prendergast's eyes widened. "It does. I suppose I owe you an apology, Ms. Weston. I've underestimated you."

Rosie flushed. "Don't worry about it. I rarely meet passengers. Your equipment looks fascinating."

Dr. Prendergast gave Rosie a genuine smile this time. "You're the train's mechanic, aren't you?"

Rosie turned her gaze downward. "Fireman, but yes. When I'm not shoveling coal, I'm fixing the train or learning how to drive it."

"Is that why you drew the device in your book?" At Rosie's confused expression, Dr. Prendergast added, "I saw your schematic. You have a clever mind."

Heat rushed to Rosie's cheeks. "Thank you."

Dr. Prendergast gave her an appraising look. "You remind me of an assistant I once had. Unfortunately, we had to part ways. If you grow weary of your work, call on me." She handed Rosie a crisp, white business card.

Rosie beamed and delicately placed the card in her logbook. "Thank you so much!" Her smile froze as a thought came unbidden to her. She frantically reached for her pocket watch. 1:40 am. "Damn! Honora's going to kill me. I'm sorry, but I need you to return to your compartment."

"Of course. Have a good night." Dr. Prendergast swept out of the baggage car.

Rosie pocketed her logbook and headed back to the cab, whistling a cheerful tune.

Honora was not impressed with Rosie's tale as they navigated the sharp turn. She had barely made it back in time. Out of breath, she told Honora all about the strange encounter with Dr. Prendergast.

"She sounds odd." Honora drank deeply from a steaming mug of coffee.

"I think she's wonderful."

"You would, kid." Honora rolled her eyes.

"I'm nearly twenty."

Rosie was spared whatever biting comeback Honora had when red light shined into the driver's compartment. She rushed to her post. The conductor was frantically waving his lantern. "Emergency stop," she told Honora, but she was already sounding the emergency whistle for the brakeman. Rosie quickly signaled with her own lantern, letting the conductor know they saw his warning.

"Brace yourself!" Honora pulled the emergency brake. Several terrible moments passed while the train clanged and bumped to a halt. Miraculously, the train didn't derail. Honora and Rosie peered at the tracks. There wasn't anything blocking their path. The engineer frowned. "Go find out what's wrong. Something feels off."

Rosie turned to leave, but much to her surprise, Honora handed her a worn jacket. "Here. No need for you to catch pneumonia."

"Thank you. I'll be back soon." Rosie put on the jacket and tucked a wayward black curl into her red headscarf.

Honora nodded and returned to her post.

The conductor and brakeman usually rode in one of the last cars. Rosie was fully prepared to trek to the back of the train. When she opened the door to the baggage car, she collided with Patrick Hand, the conductor.

"Sorry, sir. Didn't expect you to be here. What's the problem?"

Patrick looked down at his now damp uniform and sighed. The conductor had sharp cheekbones and a velvety voice. His uniform was always pristine. Rosie thought he would be better suited for vaudeville than conducting, but she didn't dare say so.

Shaking his head, Patrick cleared his throat. "We have a passenger missing. Bennie Olaughlin left for the ladies' lavatory thirty minutes ago. Her husband, Bill, alerted the porter after she didn't return. The porter says there's no sign she ever entered the lavatory."

"Oh, no! Do you need help finding her?" As sad as the situation was, Rosie was confused. There were plenty of Pullman porters to help with the search, though most would be asleep at this hour.

"Perhaps. Mr. Olaughlin thought perhaps his wife had gotten lost, as she's prone to do. I would have thought the same, given their ages, but-" Patrick took a quick breath and the next part came out quickly. "Some passengers say they heard strange noises in the aisles. No one has seen anything, though."

"What?"

"There's more." Patrick's mouth was set in a grim line. He stepped aside, allowing Rosie to see the cargo side of the car. Trunks and machines were strewn everywhere. Rosie's gaze landed on Dr. Prendergast's peculiar cargo and gasped. The chain was shattered. The trunk was open.

Ignoring Patrick's questions, Rosie hurried over to the trunk. The inside was lined with cream-colored satin ruined by slash marks. Blocks of partially melted ice were spaced around the edges of the interior. Inexplicably, a small pillow rested at one end of the trunk. For the first time, Rosie noticed the small holes drilled into the lid. The image of a coffin with air holes came to mind. Her stomach churned.

"Did you notice anything odd when you fixed the generator earlier?"

"Well, yes." Rosie was shaken, but she told Patrick about Dr. Prendergast. When she finished, she said, "But she left before I did. I made sure to lock everything up before I went back to the cab."

Patrick's face blanched. "I want you to locate Dr. Prendergast and find out what was in the trunk. I need to help the porters find Mrs. Olaughlin."

"Then what?"

The conductor's face darkened. "Find me."

Rosie left the baggage car alone. He wanted to examine Dr. Prendergast's trunk more thoroughly before continuing the search for Mrs. Olaughlin. The door to the dining car was left open, but everything else remained undisturbed. This was enough to prompt Rosie to take a butcher knife from the kitchen and store it carefully in her tool belt. It wasn't like Patrick to leave the car doors open. She was on high alert as she made her way to the passenger cars.

The lavish interior of the lounge car made Rosie feel self-conscious, though it was empty. The formerly pristine oriental rug running the length of the floor was ruined by her dirty boots. She took care to not touch any of the damask-patterned furniture as she crept past. Her foot connected with a bump in the rug, and Rosie stumbled. She glanced down. It looked like someone had bunched up the carpet. Instinctively, her hand wrapped around the knife in her tool belt. The door to the first passenger car was smashed on one edge.

Grunting, Rosie struggled to open the damaged door to the first passenger car. When the door finally slid open, she bit back a scream. The inside of her cheek throbbed, and she could taste copper. A hulking figure stood in the middle of the aisle, its back to the Rosie as it peered into the sleeper compartments. The creature wore a crudely stitched, mismatched tunic made of old cotton flour sacks. Sticking out of the ill-fitting outfit were elongated mechanical limbs crisscrossed by hydraulic hoses filled with a dark liquid, reminiscent of blood mixed with oil.

The door squeaked as Rosie attempted to make her escape, alerting the monster to her presence. It whirled around and Rosie wanted to scream again. The lower half of its ash-colored face was covered with a leather muzzle. Several angry bruises dotted its forehead.

The creature's yellow, bloodshot eyes met Rosie's. It lumbered forward, its massive boots thundering down the aisle. Small compressors hissed, pumping the fluid through the hoses as it moved. Passengers woke and screamed, retreating into their sleeper compartments as the monster charged at Rosie.

Rosie's back hit the corner of the door frame hard as she backed away from the creature. The monster reached out a twisted mechanical arm. She let out a piercing scream and slashed at its arm with the butcher knife. Before its misshapen fingers could close around Rosie's shoulders, it crumpled to the floor with a heavy thud. A syringe stuck out of its back. Dr. Prendergast stood over the prone creature's body.

"I told you to sleep on the train," Dr. Prendergast said to the creature sternly. The creature let out a muffled snore.

Rosie thought she would piss herself. With a shaking finger, she pointed to the monster. "What is that?"

Dr. Prendergast sniffed. "She is the first of her kind. Mechanical heart, lungs, and appendages. The technology I used to resurrect her will save many lives. With proper funding, I could have the freedom to perfect the design. Next time, I'll be able to refine the limb length. It seems my calculations were a bit off." The doctor shook her head. "No matter. This is only a prototype."

Rosie swayed on the spot. "Only a prototype?"

Dr. Prendergast snorted. "Of course! Did you not see how clumsy she still is?"

Rosie was at a loss for words. The door behind her slid open with a screech. Patrick stepped into the car. He looked from the creature to Dr. Prendergast. "What the devil is going on?" Without waiting for an answer, he turned his fury towards the doctor. "Are you Dr. Prendergast?"

"Yes, I am."

"Right. I'm assuming this is your creation?" He pointed to the creature.

"Yes, unfortunately." Dr. Prendergast grimaced.

"I'm placing both of you in custody until we reach the station. I've seen your equipment. The police will want to talk to you." Patrick shook his head. "How in the hell it was cleared to be on the train is beyond me."

"Pay your laborers better and maybe it wouldn't be so easy to bribe them," muttered Dr. Prendergast.

"What? It doesn't matter. I need to get you both secure so I can go back to looking for Mrs. Olaughlin. Rosie, can you assist me?" Patrick grunted as he struggled to lift the creature.

"A missing passenger, I take it?" Dr. Prendergast narrowed her shrewd eyes over her lowered spectacles.

"Yes, not that it's any of your concern."

"I'm afraid it is." The doctor pointed to her work. "This creature is of my design, and now I fear it may have a fatal flaw." Dr. Prendergast shook her head sadly. "It must be the brain. I wonder if it has decayed. At any rate, I believe the fate of your missing person may be linked to my creature if they crossed paths. My creation is remarkably strong. It wouldn't take anything for her to throw a person overboard."

Bile rose in Rosie's throat. "Why would she kill a little old lady?"

"Who knows what goes on in her head? She's a damaged prototype."

Patrick ran his fingers through his mussed hair. "What a mess. Poor Mrs. Olaughlin. I'll inform her husband of the situation. Rosie, if you would be so kind as to grab the other arm?" He scowled at Dr. Prendergast. "I strongly suggest you follow willingly."

The doctor rolled her eyes. "Yes, I will come along quietly."

It was a long trek back to the baggage car after Patrick found a porter to talk to the distraught Mr. Olaughlin. The heavy creature's metal arms poked through Rosie's borrowed jacket, but with the help from the conductor, they laid the creature down inside the car.

Dr. Prendergast kept her word and followed quietly. Patrick bound the creature with spare ropes stored with the cargo. Much to Rosie's surprise, he also bound the doctor's wrists.

"I'll keep watch here. Inform Honora what has happened and get the train running again. Leave your lantern here so I can signal you." Patrick sighed. "I suppose we should telegraph the station and inform them about why we're delayed."

"I'll take care of it." Rosie paused before opening the door. Turning back to face Dr. Prendergast, she asked, "Why did you do it?"

Dr. Prendergast gave Rosie a nonplussed look. "Why did I do what, exactly?"

"Why did you build a creature? I thought your work was to help people."

"My dear girl, that is exactly the point of the creature. If I can bring back the dead with artificial limbs, hearts, and organs, think of how much more I could do for the living. This is only the beginning!" The doctor's eyes shone with a fanatic light.

Bile rose in Rosie's throat. She slammed the baggage car door behind her, rattling its hinges.

After Rosie woke the telegrapher to send a message to the station, she returned to the cab. The haunted expression on her face convinced Honora of the truth when she informed the engineer about the events since stopping the train. Honora listened, mouth agape, before they started the train back up. It wasn't easy getting the great steam engine back to speed in the pelting rain and wind, but soon enough, the train rumbled down the tracks as if nothing had ever happened.

Rosie barely uttered a word after telling Honora of all that occurred. She focused all her energy into shoveling coal. Now that they were going at a steady rate, she kept vigil with the engineer, watching the tracks, though her mind was elsewhere.

Honora cleared her throat with a low-rumbling grunt. "Do you want to talk about it more?"

The memory of the creature's fearsome visage came to the forefront of Rosie's mind. "No, thank you."

"If you change your mind, I'm here." She handed Rosie a steaming mug of coffee. "Drink this."

The numbness Rosie felt in her bones thawed. "Thank you." The heat of the coffee was a balm to her stiff hands. She sipped the coffee slowly.

Light danced in Rosie's peripheral vision. She raced back to her post. The yellow lantern light moved erratically in the baggage car. Over the wind and rain, frantic gunshots rang out.

"Stop the train. Patrick's in trouble!"

Honora obliged. Rosie signaled the brakeman, then grabbed her shovel.

"What the hell do you think you're doing?"

"I told you how big the creature is. Unless you have a weapon, this is the best I have. The butcher knife was useless."

The color drained from Honora's face. "No, I don't have a weapon. Rosie, you can't be serious. You're going to get yourself killed."

"I have to try. The creature's limbs run on hydraulics. I only need to hit the right hoses, and I can slow her down. It's our only chance."

Honora shook her head. "You're too clever for your own good. Be careful."

"I will be."

Outside the cab, Rosie braced herself. Her stomach churned as she climbed the tender.

Rosie slowly slid the door open to the baggage car. Patrick was slumped against a wall on the cargo side, either unconscious or dead. A six-shooter lay on the floor next to him. She fervently hoped he was only knocked out.

In the opposite corner, Dr. Prendergast was barricading herself behind a stack of trunks. The creature struggled to move the luggage out of the way with her twisted mechanical arms. One metal hand dangled uselessly. Her wrist was broken, and a single hose kept the hand connected.

Seeing the creature was distracted by her single-minded determination to get to the doctor, Rosie hopped the barrier to the cargo side and charged. With a single strike from her shovel, she hit the creature in a key hose near her knee. The creature let out a muffled scream, and her damaged leg crumpled. Rosie readied her shovel to strike again when the monster faced her.

Pain and fury mixed in the creature's baleful eyes. She raised an arm. Rosie shielded herself with the shovel and squeezed her eyes shut. When the impact didn't occur, Rosie opened her eyes. Using the frayed ends of her broken mechanical arm, the monster cut her leather muzzle off, revealing lips the same shade of ash as her skin. The creature stretched her mouth gingerly. Rosie could only watch in terrified silence.

"Finally." The creature's voice was low and hoarse. "Girl, stop hitting me with your shovel. I bear you no ill will. My ire is for my creator, not you."

"No!" Dr. Prendergast shouted. Angry red splotches appeared on her cheeks.

"What about poor Mrs. Olaughlin?" Rosie's voice cracked, but she held her ground.

"Who?"

"The missing passenger."

"You mean the poor soul my so-called master pushed overboard when she discovered my escape?" The creature looked murderous again. "Let me deal with Dr. Prendergast. She has more blood on her hands than you know."

"What?"

"Everything I did was to protect you! If you had been discovered before the fair, they would have had you destroyed! This is all your fault. You shouldn't have tried to escape!" The doctor pointed a bony finger at the creature.

"I did her no harm. I was escaping you. You drugged and killed that frail woman. My conscience is clear. Your soul, however, is forever tainted. You must face justice."

"Never!"

"You cannot escape!" The creature knocked the stack of trunks over. Her arm hemorrhaged dark fluid, staining her tunic. The creature loomed over Dr. Prendergast.

"Get away from me, foul, useless creature! You could have been perfect. Now look at you. You're broken. No one will fix you." Dr. Prendergast sneered.

"I was your assistant. How could you do this to me?" The creature wailed. Her shoulders slumped.

"I needed a fresh body, and you wouldn't help me get one. The problem solved itself."

Rosie's blood ran cold as she remembered Dr. Prendergast's complimentary words. "You would have done the same to me!"

As if noticing Rosie for the first time, the doctor's eyes widened. "Of course, I wouldn't have. You could have helped me perfect her."

The creature roared and put Dr. Prendergast into a choke hold. The doctor's face turned purple.

"Wait!" Rosie stepped forward, lightly touching the creature's arm. It was hot to the touch.

"Why? She doesn't deserve mercy."

"No, she doesn't. You don't want blood on your hands, do you?"

The creature relaxed her hold on the doctor. "I do not."

Rosie studied the creature's face. "You once had a name, right?"

"Lucille." She frowned. "I cannot remember my surname, only fragments of my past. Nuns raised me in an orphanage. The doctor took me in. She promised me a better life in exchange for my help. When she was unsatisfied with my work, she murdered me for her experiments."

Rosie's blood boiled. "Let Dr. Prendergast face justice the right way."

"Very well. I shall submit myself to justice, too." Lucille let go of the gasping doctor. Inspecting her arms, she added, "If I don't bleed out first."

"I can probably fix that," Rosie offered. She stepped forward, but Dr. Prendergast was faster. The doctor lunged forward with a syringe.

"You'll do no such thing!" Dr. Prendergast's syringe hit its mark. Lucille fell forward.

"No!" Rosie swung her shovel at the doctor's head, knocking her out.

She rushed to Lucille's side to remove the syringe from her torso. "What'd she give you?" Rosie asked, not expecting an answer.

"Knockout drug," Lucille yawned, then passed out.

Rosie surveyed the room. Patrick, Dr. Prendergast, and Lucille were all unconscious. Breathing hard, Rosie checked Patrick's pulse. He would live. So would Dr. Prendergast, but Rosie wasn't sure she cared. Finally, she came to Lucille. Blood pooled around her knee and arms. Her breathing was labored.

Rosie tore through Dr. Prendergast's trunks. Luckily, she found the parts she needed. Working fast, Rosie patched up the pneumatic hoses and reattached Lucille's hand. It wasn't her best work, but it was good enough. She hissed in Lucille's ear, "Wake up!"

Lucille slowly opened her eyes. When her eyes focused again, she frowned. "Why are you helping me?"

"You deserve better." Rosie helped Lucille up. "Can you walk?"

Warily, Lucille stood. She took a few steps. "I believe so."

"Good. There isn't much time. I'll help you if you'd like. I have a plan, but I need you to hide."

Lucille stared at Rosie, then at Dr. Prendergast, who

was prone on the floor, her elegant clothes rumpled. "What must I do?"

By the time Patrick and Dr. Prendergast woke, Lucille was gone, and the rain had stopped.

"Where is the monster?" Patrick looked wildly around the car.

"She has a name. Lucille's gone. I couldn't stop her," Rosie told him. Her eyes were wide and guileless.

Dr. Prendergast gave her a knowing look but said nothing.

The rest of the ride to the Chicago station was uneventful. Honora tried to talk to Rosie a few times, but Rosie told the engineer she was exhausted. Honora sulked, wanting to hear more about the creature's escape, but Rosie could tell Honora was happy to see her back safely. They drank coffee in amiable silence before bringing the train to a gentle stop.

The police were waiting for Dr. Prendergast as soon as the train pulled into the station. Rosie stared after the doctor as they escorted her. An elderly man, presumably Mr. Olaughlin, shouted and shook his gnarled fist at the silent doctor. Rosie hoped this was the last she saw of Dr. Prendergast.

Rosie had to wait hours before she could sneak back to the train. She climbed the tender, listening for any overnight workers passing by. She was alone. A lone tube barely stuck out of the coal, the only sign anything was amiss.

Rosie brushed off the light layer of coal covering Lucille's concealed body.

Lucille spat out the tube and coughed. She was completely covered in soot.

"Never again," Lucille wheezed.

"I'm so sorry. It was the only place I could think of no one would check. Are you okay?"

Lucille carefully moved her mechanical limbs. "I'm fine. What's next?"

Rosie grinned. "I'm going to smuggle you into the World's Fair. With all these inventors gathering in the same city, someone is bound to have the parts we need to fix you up."

"Thank you. It's good to have a friend."

Rosie extended her hand and helped Lucille climb out of the tender. Unnoticed by the station's watchman, the unlikely duo disappeared into the night.

THE BLOOD IS LIFE

L*ast time, our heroines narrowly escaped the clutches of the diabolical Dr. Prendergast. After smuggling Lucille off the train, Rosie will finally achieve her dream of attending the World's Fair, but their luck is running out.*

"What do you mean, Mr. Tesla isn't at the World's Fair?" Rosie brimmed with righteous indignation. Her voice carried over the crowded thoroughfare. Her cheeks tinged pink as passersby turned at her outburst. Nearby, Lucille waited next to the ornate MacMonnies Fountain. The last thing Rosie wanted was to attract attention to her incognito companion. The flashy display of high-thrown water coming out of the sculpted dolphins soon distracted the other pedestrians.

The Columbian Guard shrugged. His elaborate navy uniform made Rosie feel under-dressed in her least-stained coveralls. Even the individual buttons on his braided blouse were made to look like globes. "I'm sorry, Miss. Some of his inventions will be displayed at the Great Hall of Electricity, but I'm afraid the exhibit is incomplete."

Shaking her head, Rosie stomped over to Lucille.

"Any luck?" The newsboy cap pulled low over Lucille's face obscured her yellow eyes and made the scars crisscrossing her ashen face less pronounced. Rosie couldn't believe she had found a pair of coveralls that fit Lucille's massive frame. There was enough legroom that the compressors didn't show through the material.

"No. He's not here," Rosie grumbled, then stifled a yawn. Yesterday had been a long day and an even longer night. As soon as her fireman duties were over, Rosie smuggled most of Dr. Prendergast's equipment out of the baggage compartment. It had been a small miracle that the police hadn't already confiscated all the doctor's luggage.

After securing the trunks, she'd raced around Chicago for clothes and supplies. The hardest part had been waiting until dark so she could retrieve Lucille from the tender.

Her heart still raced from stealing the scientist's work, but it was worth it. She'd patched up Lucille as best as she could with the stolen spare parts. A laborious task not made easier by the sudden downpour that drenched them as they left the station.

Seeing her new friend up and moving after the ordeal soothed Rosie's heart, even if some of her movements were rigid and jerky. They desperately needed help to further repair the complex hydraulics making up Lucille's circulatory system.

"Who isn't here?" Lucille's low, scratchy voice brought Rosie out of her musings. From the expectant expression on her face, it was not the first time she'd asked.

"Mr. Tesla. He's not here." Rosie pulled the World's Fair flyer from her logbook and jabbed at it accusingly. "This thing lied to me! See, he's right here, on the front."

Lucille raised a thin eyebrow. "Was your entire plan based on finding Nikola Tesla at the Fair?"

"Well," Rosie snapped the logbook shut on the flyer. "Not exactly." She knocked a clump of mud from her well-worn boots.

"It will be okay," Lucille said, smiling. "You told me this event would be full of inventors. Let's find someone else who can help us."

"You're right." Rosie's stomach rumbled loudly. Her cheeks flushed.

"After we find something for you to eat."

"Good plan." They walked in amicable silence for a few steps. "It occurred to me that I never asked if you still eat."

"Of course, I require food. I'm still human." Lucille bristled, tensing up her shoulders. "But I need to be cautious about what I ingest. Certain foods are more difficult for me to process."

The pair walked through the crowded path through the center of the Fair after grabbing a bite to eat at one of the lunch counters. Lucille's hydraulic compressors hissed with each movement, but the noise was swallowed by the passersby in awe of the White City. The buildings were neoclassical with gleaming white facades. Exhibits stretched to the horizon, with more pavilions being built. The great Ferris wheel in the center of the Midway was far from completion.

Rosie couldn't bring herself to enjoy the sights.

Each time a brunette walked by, her heart pounded. She had no idea if Dr. Prendergast was still in custody. There had been no time this morning to check the paper to see if the incident on the train was reported or if the railway had kept the story quiet. She hoped the stories about the World's Fair buried other news.

Lucille was doing the best she could to blend in, but

with her height, it was difficult. She tried giving a wide berth to the other fairgoers, but the crowds pressed in on all sides.

Rosie was accustomed to strangers staring at her bronze and white vitiligo, but now she felt paranoid if anyone's gaze lingered for more than a moment.

The feeling someone was following them permeated Rosie's thoughts. She had caught no one when she checked over her shoulder, but the hairs on the back of her neck stood on end. Her inquisitive glances were met by a few polite, bemused smiles, but most fairgoers frowned and went about their business. It set Rosie's teeth on edge, but she kept her fears to herself. There was no need to worry Lucille.

Finding help was proving impossible. By midday, both of them were irritable. They could explore the Exposition Buildings, but they couldn't get close to any of the inventors presenting. Often, a wonderful invention would be on display, but the creator would be absent. When an inventor was present, the excitable audience would make it impossible to approach the presenter. Worse, many of the attractions cost money. Rosie's face fell every time she had to take from her dwindling funds.

Fed up, Lucille stomped away from the latest attraction that wanted to charge each of them a quarter. Rosie had to jog to catch up to the other woman's long stride.

"Lucille! Wait!" Rosie panted as they reached the gates. "Where are you going?"

Lucille's shoulders drooped. "Rosie, this isn't working. We're getting nowhere. We keep spending your money. My joints are aching. I haven't been this active since waking up in Dr. Prendergast's lab. I need rest."

Rosie bit her tongue, thinking about the price of admission she had paid. "Maybe we could find somewhere for you to sit while I keep looking. There's got to be someone here who can help us."

Lucille shook her head sadly. "I appreciate everything you've done. Truly, I do. But I fear I should have parted ways with you after the train. I don't want to be a burden. You should go enjoy the Fair. It's been your dream to attend. I'll head back to the hotel and rest for a bit."

Rosie stood motionless as Lucille lumbered out of the entryway, back into the crowded streets of Chicago. Her heart longed to listen to Lucille's advice and enjoy the Fair.

With a heavy sigh, Rosie turned her back on the exposition. It didn't take long to catch up with Lucille, who was waiting to cross a busy intersection.

"What are you doing?" Lucille rumbled when Rosie tapped on her arm.

"I'm coming with you. I'm worried about you."

Lucille rolled her eyes. "No, you're not. After I rest, I'm leaving. I don't want to be anyone's burden!"

The traffic was thundering chaos. Phaetons, victorias, omnibuses, and other experimental automobiles raced down the busy street. Drivers shouted and rang gongs as they buzzed past frightened pedestrians who strayed too close.

"I can't let you go like this! You still need-" Rosie stopped short of saying repairs, "help. Better help than I can give you. This is dangerous. And She," her hands fluttered frantically as she danced around saying Dr. Prendergast's name aloud, "could still be out there."

Lucille's bloodshot eyes narrowed. "I can deal with 'her' if the need arises."

"You shouldn't have to go through this alone!" Rosie shouted, straining to be heard over the racket. Nearby pedestrians gave her disapproving looks.

"You need to let me go," Lucille replied, turning away. The crowd bustled too close, bumping into her. The sudden movement upset her balance a fraction too far, and she was jostled off the curb. Her eyes widened. For the briefest of moments, her eyes locked with Rosie's.

With a sickening crunch, an overcrowded omnibus crashed into Lucille. She crumpled.

Rosie screamed.

"Lucille!"

Rosie rushed to Lucille's side to pull her out of the oncoming traffic. The omnibus careened away, the driver oblivious to the crash. Traffic rushed by, with shouting for Rosie to get out of the way, adding to the cacophony. No one stopped to help. A few pedestrians stared as they crossed the street or turned the corner to walk down the block.

All Rosie could see was Lucille, unconscious and bleeding through her clothes. Her limbs bent at unnatural angles. She needed to get both of them back to the hotel for supplies, but it was a lengthy walk. Much too far away to carry her friend.

Rosie kneeled, resting Lucille's head in her lap as much as possible. She leaned forward and hissed into her ear, "Lucille? Can you hear me? Wake up!"

Lucille didn't stir.

Rosie placed two fingers along a raised section on Lucille's neck, where she knew a hydraulic hose carried the mysterious black fluid like a vein carrying blood.

She couldn't feel a pulse.

Rosie leaned closer to listen for signs of breathing. It was impossible over the din of noise. Indifferent passersby bumped into her. Cold sweat dotted Rosie's forehead as her heart hammered. She placed a hand on

Lucille's stomach. The other woman's chest rose and fell with each breath. Rosie allowed herself a small sigh of relief.

"Do you need help?" A man's voice came from behind Rosie.

Without turning around, she kept looking for the source of the leaking hose. "I need to stop the bleeding." She struggled to roll up Lucille's soaked trouser leg, her hands slick with the leaking dark fluid. The metal pieces forming the artificial left leg were bent and twisted out of shape, further complicating matters.

Rosie removed the red headscarf she wore to keep her riotous black curls at bay. With shaking hands, she created a makeshift tourniquet around the punctured hose with the scarf. It was immediately stained an oily black, but the bleeding slowed.

The stranger kneeled beside Rosie. Her shoulders tensed at his proximity. She waited for him to ask about Lucille's mechanical limbs.

So far, none of the witnesses had commented about how different Lucille was, from her ash-colored skin or the metal pieces sticking out of her trouser leg. Rosie glanced at the man, always keeping Lucille in her line of sight.

He was dapper, like Patrick the conductor. Likely dyed his perfectly coiffed hair like the conductor, too, based on his crow's feet. His suit was pressed and spotless. His shoes were probably spotless too, despite the muck, but she didn't care enough to check.

The stranger smiled. His teeth were unnaturally white, sunlight glinting off his teeth. "Allow me to introduce myself. I'm Albin Morris, chemist. Can I help you get your friend to the hospital?"

Rosie panicked. If she took her to the hospital, they would quickly find out Lucille's secrets. Rosie wondered if they would figure out she'd escaped from the train. All her fears about Dr. Prendergast rose to the surface. What would happen to Lucille if her creator found her?

Rosie gulped. "N-no thank you. No hospitals. My friend has delicate prosthetics and requires specialized care." Internally, she screamed. She didn't know how to move Lucille without furthering the damage.

"I see." Mr. Morris gestured to the surrounding crowd. "Then may I suggest the use of my shop? It's only a brief streetcar ride to the west."

Rosie chewed her bottom lip and looked down at Lucille. She looked paler now. Rosie fervently wished Lucille were awake so she could ask her what she wanted to do.

"People are noticing." Mr. Morris' voice was low and hushed.

Rosie looked up. Sure enough, a few curious onlookers were looking in their direction. She winced.

"It appears I have little choice. Led the way."

Rosie's arms burned and ached as Mr. Morris helped her half-drag, half-carry Lucille into his chemist shop. The sign read above the chemist shop looked as if it had been freshly painted. It read, "Mr. Morris' Emporium of Elixirs, Established in 1852."

The door opened with the gentle tingling of a bell. Rosie maneuvered Lucille into the shop, being careful to not bash her delicate limbs into the door frame.

Inside, there were rows upon rows of tinctures and elixirs that promised everything from curing gout to reducing wrinkles to eliminating coughs. There was a dizzying array of shelves and endless drawers that must have contained enough medicine to stock a hospital. She wondered briefly if there would be anything in stock that could help Lucille, but without knowing the composition of the artificial blood, it would be dangerous to experiment.

Mr. Morris picked Lucille up by her ankles. "I have a workroom in the back. The table should be sturdy enough to hold her." He grimaced as he readjusted his grip. "Emphasis on 'should' hold her weight."

They knocked over a tonic on the counter before laying Lucille on top of the metal work table. It was clear of any experiments or paperwork, unlike the rest of the cluttered room, and it was long enough for the unconscious woman's tall frame.

"Do you have anything I can use to stop the bleeding?" Rosie's chest tightened as she spotted fresh black stains blooming on Lucille's clothes. "She has more leaks than I thought."

"Let me go check. I should have just the thing you need."

Mr. Morris disappeared into a closet. Rosie used the time to listen to Lucille's breathing again. It remained steady, but she worried it was still shallow. While he was gone, she took advantage of the privacy to roll up Lucille's sleeves and trouser legs.

The source of the new leaks was easy enough to find. Luckily, some hoses were only displaced, not cut, and Rosie reinserted the hoses where they had slipped out. It was the severed section that was posing the problem.

Her headscarf was completely drenched. Rosie experimented with tying it tighter, but it only seemed to block the flow of the liquid rather than prevent further leaking. Her fingernails were stained with the black fluid.

Mr. Morris returned with towels and a variety of tubing.

"They're not perfect, but might do in a pinch." He sat

the hoses down next to Lucille on the work table. He stared at her exposed limbs.

Rosie was prepared to tell several lies to stave off on any inquiries. It surprised her when all he murmured was, "Breathtaking detail on her limbs. Remarkable."

Rosie didn't know how to respond, so she examined the tubing Mr. Morris had brought. She found one close enough to the width of Lucille's hoses and cut it down to size.

"Can you pinch this part of the hose here? I'll rig up a temporary fix." Rosie pointed to the soaked headscarf.

"Of course." Mr. Morris held onto the scarf, never taking his eyes off the hose.

Rosie worked quickly, afraid the hose would sputter and spurt across the room. She barely could fit the new hose inside the original tubing.

"Okay, you can let go slowly. Let's see if this works."

With bated breath, Rosie watched as the blood flowed smoothly from the original hose through the new section. It wasn't a perfect fit, and the moment Lucille was mobile it would likely pop out, but for now, it was working.

After several minutes passed, more color returned to Lucille's face, though Rosie noted with despair she still didn't quite look right.

"Is she always this pale?" Mr. Morris asked, breaking the silence.

"No. I mean, her skin is usually gray like soot, not steam cloud gray," Rosie said absently. She studied the tubes flowing down Lucille's arms. The fluid was too clear. "Dammit, she's lost too much blood. I need the spare vials."

Mr. Morris raised an inquisitive brow. "Come again?"

Rosie chewed her lip before responding carefully. "I have spare equipment for Lucille's special prosthetics and her unique blood type back at our lodgings. I need to get her to the supplies so I can repair her, but I don't think I can move her in this state."

"I can keep watch over your friend."

Rosie looked down at Lucille, then back to Mr. Morris. As much as she hated leaving Lucille with this stranger, she had to get the supplies.

"Keep a close eye on her. I'll be back as soon as I can."

Mr. Morris smiled, his teeth gleaming in the gaslight lamps. "You have my word."

Rosie double checked the chemist's shop address as she wrote it down in her logbook. Her stomach churned as she set off for the hotel alone.

Rosie took a streetcar straight to the hotel. She resisted the urge to keep checking her pocket watch as the seconds ticked by. She couldn't shake the feeling she had made a colossal mistake. Her foot tapped impatiently the entire ride, ignoring the other passengers staring at her stained hands.

When the streetcar finally reached her stop, Rosie bolted out of the car, barely stopping to have her ticket checked. She ran all the way to the hotel room, past the inquisitive glance of the front desk clerk, and up the three flights of stairs to her quarters. She scrubbed her hands as best as she could.

There wasn't much storage space in the room, but Rosie had cleverly hidden the supplies she nicked, terrified the hotel staff would grow inquisitive if they saw anything suspicious.

It had taken her hours and a lot of sneaking around to move the equipment, but she knew repairing Lucille would be unfeasible without the parts. It was fortunate the station was so busy. Everyone had too much work to do to pay attention to a lone fireman.

She hadn't stolen all of Dr. Prendergast's equipment, but enough that she hoped she could keep Lucille maintained until she could find a more long-term solution.

The first trunk was stashed under the bed, beneath Rosie's spare clothes. She removed three vials of the viscous black-red solution that served as Lucille's blood. She still didn't know what the fluid was made of, but she was glad to have spare vials. The exposed hydraulic hoses on Lucille's limbs made Rosie nervous for her friend. She wanted a covering for the tubing, anything to keep Lucille from walking around with her man-made veins exposed.

The spare hoses were kept above the doorframe of the tiny washroom. Rosie had to jump to reach it.

Finally, Rosie opened the steamer trunk near the window. After removing clothes and blankets, she lifted the false bottom to reveal the various sizes of the metal pieces used for Lucille's limbs. The spare parts resembled silver, mechanical bones. She pocketed several extra bolts. Rosie locked the trunk, then placed her pile of equipment in the middle of the room. She grabbed an oversized worn knapsack to toss everything in. As an afterthought, she also packed a change of clothes for Lucille, using it to wrap the delicate vials.

Before leaving, Rosie scrubbed her hands once more and put on a fresh headscarf. Trembling, she retrieved a pocketknife from the nightstand, a recent purchase from her supply run, and added it to her tool belt. She took several deep, grounding breaths before heading back to Mr. Morris' shop. She prayed she'd be fast enough.

Rosie was sweating profusely when she pushed the door open into Mr. Morris' Emporium of Elixirs. Despite the heavy equipment, she made it back quickly.

The chemist sat on a stool next to the work table Lucille laid on. A clear hose ran between the two. Rosie's eyes widened as she realized there was blood in the tube. Was the chemist giving Lucille a blood transfusion? Rosie silently crept further into the room as she kept her eyes on the hose. Black fluid ran through the clear tubing. It was Lucille's blood flowing into Mr. Morris.

"Get away from her!" Rosie rushed forward and punched Mr. Morris in the jaw. Her fist hit him with a satisfying crack.

"Take the tubes out. Now." Rosie glared at the chemist. "I'll rip them out of your arm myself if you don't."

"As you wish," Mr. Morris sniffed, rubbing his jaw. He took out the needles and disconnected Lucille from the hose. "It's not as if she's in any real danger."

Rosie decked him again.

The chemist landed hard on his backside. "That was entirely uncalled for."

Rosie let out a hollow laugh. "You gave me your word, then you violated my trust by draining her limited blood. How dare you!"

"I would not take enough to harm her." Somehow, even with the purple bruises blooming on his jawline, Mr. Morris looked indignant sitting on the hardwood floor. "By rights, she should be dead already. Or are you going to tell me you didn't notice?"

Her expression hardened. "You had no right to touch her." She leaned over Lucille to check her breathing. It was faint, but steady. The fluid in her hydraulics was running almost completely clear.

Rosie placed herself between Mr. Morris and Lucille, blocking his view. She frantically pulled one vial from her knapsack. She unbuttoned Lucille's shirt enough to see the screw-on cap directly below her collarbone, marked by an arcane symbol in front of a red teardrop. Rosie removed the cap and poured in the vial. She screwed the cap back on tightly, being careful to not strip it out. Color returned to Lucille's face. Rosie breathed a sigh of relief before turning her fury on Mr. Morris.

"What the hell were you thinking?"

"I'm a scientist. Naturally, I was curious about the artificial blood. I wanted to test it out." Mr. Morris fidgeted, his eyes darting back to Lucille's exposed hoses.

"By injecting it into yourself? You shouldn't have been experimenting without Lucille's consent. This is wrong!"

"You don't understand." A maniacal grin spread on the chemists' face. "I've toiled for years to solve humanity's last problem. Did you not wonder about the elixirs in my shop? My chemical solutions have restored my youth. And now, with this miraculous creature's blood, I may have unlocked the ultimate key to immortality. Her miraculous blood has granted her new life at least once before."

"You had no right." Rosie shook her head. "You're going to get yourself killed."

"Ah, but did you have the right to smuggle her off the train? Or steal her creator's belongings?" An ugly sneer crossed Mr. Morris' face. "The evening paper last night had an article about an unearthly creature terrorizing the passengers of a train on the way to the World's Fair. I counted my lucky stars when I saw the two of you wandering about the grounds."

Rosie's heart sank. Who else would figure out Lucille's identity?

He let his words sink in, then he drove the dagger home. "If you strike me again, I'll go to the authorities. I've been a respected member of this community for decades. They'll take one look at you and lock you up."

Mr. Morris' grin was predatory. "Do we have an understanding?"

Rosie contemplated escape, but they both knew she couldn't move Lucille alone.

"Fine. If you touch Lucille, I will punch you again, the authorities be damned. Do we have an understanding?"

"We have an accord. I'll sit in the corner while you work. I'm interested in Lucille's progress."

Rosie couldn't help but think of a snake slithering away as he took a seat.

"Yeah, you would, you bastard." Rosie set about repairing a compressor on Lucille's right leg. She worked in silence for several minutes until her grip slipped and caught her finger on a sharp edge. Expletives flew from her mouth. A paper-thin cut appeared on her left index finger. She wrapped it with the spare gauze she kept in her tool belt.

With a reassuring click, she reconnected the hose and tightened the bolts holding the compressor in place. Confident of her work, she checked Lucille over for any damage she missed.

A loud metal scraping noise made Rosie snarl. "What now?" She gasped when she looked up.

Mr. Morris was effortlessly lifting another heavy work table on the other side of the room. He didn't break a sweat as he raised and lowered it again.

"It seems Lucille's blood was good for me." Mr. Morris gently set the workstation down. His eyes lit up. "But she would need extra strength to bear the weight of her metal arms."

"I don't know if I would say it's good for you." Rosie could see even at a distance the blackened veins that stretched from Mr. Morris' fingertips to above his rolled-up sleeve.

"Nonsense. I'm perfectly fine."

Rosie went back to ignoring the chemist and tightened the last of the hoses. She waited with bated breath to see if her efforts would be enough.

"I feel like all my thoughts are happening at once. Marvelous!" Mr. Morris frenetically scribbled notes on a chalkboard on the back wall, correcting errors in complex chemical equations written on the board.

"Shut up." Rosie wrinkled her nose.

Lucille slowly opened her eyes and coughed. "Rosie?" she asked, her voice hoarse.

Rosie gave Lucille a relieved smile. "Can I give you a hug?"

An oily tear streaked across Lucille's ashen face. "Of course."

The mechanical limbs dug into Rosie's side as she embraced Lucille, but she didn't mind.

From his corner in the lab, Mr. Morris groaned. "Something doesn't feel right."

He collapsed with a thud.

Mr. Morris' slight frame quivered as he spasmed on the floor of his backroom. Rosie watched with mounting horror as his muscles and sinew undulated wildly. His skin bubbled and grew. His suit tore along the seams as his muscles rippled. All his veins were visibly black through his sickly jaundiced skin. With twisting, jerky movements, he shakily rose, bending at unnatural angles. His torso bent backwards. With a mighty crack, he stood up straight.

Rosie screamed.

Instead of the well-manicured, reedy man Rosie met earlier, now Mr. Morris resembled a hulking, hairless ape wearing a tattered suit. His arms were long enough to drag his knuckles on the floor. His hands were four times their natural size. Hair fell out in clumps, left scattered on the floor by his feet. His muscles rivaled the strongman at the Midway. He stretched his enormous mouth wide and smiled. His teeth were crooked and loose from his jaw's rapid expansion.

Bile rose in Rosie's throat.

"What is that?" Lucille pointed, her mechanical finger twitching.

"You wound me." Mr. Morris' once smooth voice was now a mangled growl. "I'm the man who rescued you. And now I'm like you. We're the only two of our kind in the world. At last, the secret of immortality will be mine." He enthusiastically pounded his fist into the floor, punctuating his sentence.

"He did something weird with your blood," hissed Rosie, never taking her eyes off the monstrosity before her. "He injected it into himself."

"You fool," Lucille thundered. "You do not understand what sort of dangerous alchemy was used to bring me back to life."

Mr. Morris' lip twisted cruelly. "So, I was right about your origin. Surely, more secrets run in your artificial veins." He stretched out his oversized hand. "Join me, and together we can unravel the mystery."

"You want to spend eternity looking like this?" Lucille gestured to her scarred skin and metal limbs.

Mr. Morris sneered. "Our appearances can always be altered later. If not, it's the sacrifice we make for the greater good."

Rosie shook her head. "You can't be serious."

"It's not worth it," Lucille said quietly but firmly.

"So be it, then. I don't need your cooperation to study the enigmas of your blood." He grinned menacingly. "In fact, your companion has more of your blood in the satchel over there." A hard glint was in his eyes. "It appears I don't need you at all."

"Grab my bag and run!" Rosie stepped protectively in front of Lucille, pulling the biggest wrench from her tool belt.

Mr. Morris advanced slowly, chuckling darkly. "Do you really think your little tool will stop me?"

Cold metal fingers delicately rested on Rosie's shoulder. She looked up to see Lucille standing next to her. "Leave this abomination to me. He'll crush you."

Rosie gritted her teeth. "Be careful. First chance you get run after me." She grabbed her knapsack and bolted for the shop's exit.

Mr. Morris lumbered after her, scraping his knuckles as he ran on all fours. As she reached the door, he violently swept her back into the store with one hand.

"No, you will witness my moment of triumph. You stay."

Rosie cracked her mouth on the wrench. She wiped the blood away and spat at the chemist. "This isn't triumph. This is madness!"

"How dare you! Insolent brat."

Mr. Morris let out a roar and raised both fists. He made to slam down his fists on Rosie, but was stopped by Lucille charging, a mass of metal and flesh running at him at full speed into his side. They crashed into the nearby table. Samples toppled over, and vials cracked. Mr. Morris slumped against the wooden cabinets.

With wobbling legs, Rosie stood up. She took several shaky steps toward the exit.

"No!" Mr. Morris pushed himself off the floor, knocking Lucille out of the way. He trudged forward.

Rosie whirled around, clenching her wrench so tightly her knuckles turned white. She waited for him to be in range, then threw. It landed solidly on Mr. Morris' forehead. He howled in pain, covering his face.

"You die now," he raged, removing his hand from his wound. Black blood flowed down his face.

Rosie flicked open her pocketknife. She squared her shoulders and calmly waited for the inevitable attack.

It never came.

Lucille rallied and threw her body weight at Mr. Morris. They grappled and wrestled across the room, crashing into test tubes and beakers.

Lucille released her grip to pick up a rack of vials and hurled them at Mr. Morris. Acid burns dotted his body and he let out a piercing scream. He lunged, then slumped forward, holding his head.

"No, it's all leaving me," he wailed. Black blood leaked from the corners of his eyes, mixing with tears.

Lucille lowered her fists.

"What do you mean?"

"My thoughts... all strength gone." His words slurred.

"We're leaving," Rosie announced, grabbing her bag.

"Shouldn't we check to see if he'll be okay?"

Rosie raised her eyebrows. "He tried to kill us."

"I know." Lucille twisted her hands.

Rosie sighed. "Fine." She kneeled next to the chemist.

"Are you done now?" She wrinkled her nose at the fetid scent coming from Mr. Morris.

"Do-ne." His voice was slow and faraway. A bit of drool pooled at the corner of his mouth.

"I think he's melted his brain."

"Mr. Morris?" Lucille asked hesitantly.

He stared blankly ahead.

"Now what?" Lucille asked, wringing her hand.

"We were never here," Rosie said flatly.

"Are you sure you're okay?" Rosie fussed for the twentieth time.

"You're the one who repaired me," rumbled Lucille as they walked towards the Exposition. Both had slept hard last night, and now they were going to the Fair properly. "Don't you have confidence in your abilities?" Her tone was teasing. She smiled at Rosie's fretting.

"Well, yes, but the last two days have been hell on your system. Are you sure you want to go back?" Guilt wrenched her as she thought about their fight. "What if someone else recognizes you?"

"We can deal with them, too, if the need arises."

"I guess."

Lucille and Rosie walked in contemplative silence for a few steps. The gates to the Fair loomed ahead.

"It would be nice to see the Exposition, even if Mr. Tesla isn't here," Rosie mused.

"See? That's the spirit."

"I saw a poster for a Living Metal Man. Should we go find you a companion?"

"You wouldn't dare!"

Rosie cackled as they walked through the gates.

THE LIVING METAL MAN

Last time, Rosie and Lucille encountered the dastardly chemist, Mr. Morris. After witnessing his terrifying transformation and subsequent demise, our heroines are determined to enjoy the World's Fair at last.

"Come on! The seats are going to all be taken." Rosie pulled Lucille by her gloved hand along the thoroughfare. It was the second day of the World's Fair. The skeletal structures of half-finished pavilions and muddy temporary construction tracks blighted the otherwise opulent landscape. Still, Rosie was buzzing with excitement as they neared the Electrical Building.

A dramatic poster of the silhouette of a humanoid automaton before a colorful crowd was plastered to the exterior of the stately building. Inside, incomplete displays contrasted starkly against the finished ones, dazzling with flashing lights and complex machinery.

The sparse crowd milling about the hall disappointed

Rosie until Lucille pointed out it would be easier on her to navigate the Exposition. The healing cut on her lip reminded Rosie fewer people would be a welcome reprieve. Her muscles ached from the confrontation with Mr. Morris yesterday, though she didn't let her stiffness curb her enthusiasm for a day at the fair.

She'd learned not to let her guard down, though. She didn't know the whereabouts of Dr. Prendergast and a careful reading of the morning paper revealed nothing about Lucille's so-called creator. It was unnerving to have no knowledge at all, but she reasoned even if the doctor were walking free, the odds of her tracking Lucille to the exposition were low.

"I thought you were joking about going to this," complained Lucille. "Slow down a little. My compressors can't keep up."

"Aren't you curious? I want to see what it's about." Rosie slowed her pace but kept going. "Look! Front row seats. It's the last two!"

"Yes, I am curious," Lucille relented as they sat down. She slouched in her seat. "But if you keep pulling on my arm, you must repair me. Again." She discreetly pulled up on the leather gloves covering her mechanical hands. "Also, I need a longer shirt. This one's a bit too short."

"I'm sorry. I'm excited to be here." Rosie's leg shook from nerves.

Lucille snorted as Rosie's knee bounced up and down.

Rosie felt heat rise in her cheeks and she held down the offending leg, causing Lucille to let out a full laugh.

"Quiet down, the show's about to start," hissed someone behind them.

"Sorry," muttered Lucille as she shrank down.

Rosie patted Lucille's hand before making a rude gesture at the complainer.

The lights in the hall dimmed. The crowd fell silent

with a hush. A stagehand lit the Edison bulbs lining the stage. Next to the lights, there were barbells, a balancing beam, and other gymnasium equipment Rosie didn't recognize.

A woman wearing an unbuttoned white coat over a shimmering aquamarine dress walked onto the stage. Another stagehand fixed a spotlight on the woman. Behind her was a seated figure, covered with a black cloth. Rosie pulled out her logbook and readied herself for note taking.

"Ladies, gentlemen, and variations thereof, welcome to The Living Metal Man, sponsored by General Electric Company! I'm Dr. Evelyn Mendel, and this is my creation." The doctor gave the crowd a dazzling smile, then pulled the cloth off the seated figure with a flourish.

A life-size silver automaton sat motionless onstage. Nothing happened for several seconds.

By his own volition, the automaton turned his head to face the spectators. "Hello," he said in a modulated voice. "My name is Adam." With a mechanical whirring sound and a few creaks, he stood and took three steps forward.

Rosie was impressed by how smooth his gait was. He stood at attention next to Dr. Mendel.

"Do I have any volunteers to inspect Adam up close?" Dr. Mendel asked.

Rosie shot her hand up so fast that Lucille had to duck.

"You, in the coveralls up front. Right this way!" Dr. Mendel beckoned to her.

Rosie beamed until the spotlight focused on her. Gulping, she tucked her logbook away and followed the stagehand to the platform.

From her seat in the hall, Rosie had thought the automaton was made of smooth sheets of aluminum cleverly welded. Up close, the level of detail amazed her. Hundreds of tiny metal plates comprised Adam's body. His compressors hummed, reminding her of Lucille's hydraulics system. Metal plates covered the hoses so she couldn't confirm her suspicion. She was dying to lift the panels on his arms to see how the system worked, but it didn't feel right with how humanoid the automaton appeared to be.

Adam stared at Rosie with guileless, doll-like eyes.

"How does he see?" Rosie asked, mesmerized.

"Selenium cells combined with a photomultiplier tube," Dr. Mendel replied.

"I've seen nothing like it."

"You have now." Dr. Mendel smiled as she handed Rosie a round hoop. "Can you show the audience there are no wires or strings around Adam?"

Rosie obliged, running the hoop over the automaton's body and each arm as he held them out straight.

"No strings here."

"What's your name?"

"Rosie." Heat rose in her cheeks. Getting on stage might not have been one of Rosie's best ideas. Her eyes darted across the audience, but the bright spotlight made it difficult to make out faces. What if Dr. Prendergast was here? Her heart pounded. She took a steadying, deep breath, reminding herself she was letting her imagination get the best of her.

"Adam, would you please shake Rosie's hand?"

"My pleasure." With a fluid motion, the automaton extended his hand.

For a terrible moment, Rosie thought he would crush her hand. Her knuckles were sore from punching the mad chemist's jaw yesterday. She hesitated before offering her own bruised and scraped hand.

As if sensing her duress, Adam's grip was gentle. "It's good to meet you."

Rosie's eyes widened when she realized how intricate the moving parts on his face were. Small plates acted as facial muscles. Adam gave her a warm, genuine smile instead of the stoic, smooth expression on his face moments before. His eyes were no longer lifeless. They shone with curiosity.

"Same to you," was all she could muster. Her mind raced with hundreds of questions. Her knees felt like they would give out. She needed to sit down.

"This is boring! Can't it do anything exciting?" called out a slurred voice from the audience.

The intense spotlight made it impossible to identify the source of the heckling. The air around Adam seemed to crackle as his shoulder joints stiffened. Rosie flinched away from the automaton.

"Hush. Adam will have plenty to show soon. I was about to explain his R.I.B. technology that allows him to have such advanced processing." Dr. Mendel's tone was pleasant, but a muscle in her cheek twitched with irritation.

Sweat pooled down Rosie's back. She regretted raising her hand. She wished she would have been able to see Adam in a lab, not on stage.

"Why doesn't it do a dance or sing a song?" another heckler called out. Several audience members jeered.

Adam's inner mechanisms buzzed at an alarming rate. His expression switched from placid to menacing. He lumbered past Rosie, but the lights overwhelmed his sensors. He crashed into the barbells, tripped, and knocked the wooden balance beam and other equipment into the Edison bulbs.

Sparks flew, and a small fire started at the front of the stage.

Members of the audience screamed. In their panicked state, they trampled over each other, racing for the exits. One brave stagehand found a bucket of water and dumped it on the fire, causing the wiring to short and crackle.

Rosie was trapped on stage with Dr. Mendel and the automaton.

As the flames rose higher, Rosie frantically searched for an exit. To her relief, the short staircase on stage left was clear.

She went back to the front of the stage, bumping into Dr. Mendel, who was pulling Adam away from the flames.

"The flames haven't reached the stairs. Do you have anything in your equipment to put out the fire?" Tears stung Rosie's eyes as she tried to focus. She hacked and coughed until she remembered the handkerchief in her back pocket. She tied it around her mouth, keeping her somewhat protected from the smoke filling the air.

"No, I'm sorry. This has never happened before." Dr. Mendel's voice cracked. "Adam, you need to wake up! You've set the stage on fire."

"Rosie!" Lucille was on the stairs, her voice muffled by her own handkerchief. "Are you all right?"

Rosie hesitated, turning back to look at Dr. Mendel and Adam. The doctor was hunched over, shielding the automaton with her body.

"Dr. Mendel!" she called out.

"Please help me get him offstage. He's too heavy." The doctor tugged at Adam's prone form with minor success.

"Okay," Rosie said, "But we need to hurry." She eyed

the spreading flames as she bent forward to help drag the automaton away from the inferno.

"Here, let me help." Lucille gently nudged Rosie aside and easily lifted Adam over her shoulders. With heavy steps thudding down the stairs, she deftly propped the automaton up against a seat in the third row.

Rosie followed, with Dr. Mendel close behind. She hoped the doctor was too grateful for the rescue of her automaton to ask questions about Lucille's supernatural strength.

Unfortunately, Rosie noticed the glint of metal peeking out from Lucille's pushed up sleeves at the same time as Dr. Mendel. The doctor gave Rosie a hard look after glancing back meaningfully at Lucille's arms.

Dr. Mendel opened her mouth to ask a question, but it died on her lips as the Fair's private firefighting brigade stormed down the hall, hose at the ready. Accompanying the brigade were two scowling men.

Their clothes were rough, as if they had just gotten off a shift at a factory, and both had scars peppering their faces, though the similarities ended there. The hirsute, burly man spoke first.

"The boss won't be happy with this," he said, clenching a cigar between his teeth. "You never responded to his last telegram."

"George, why is it you have a knack for appearing at the worst times? I can't do this now." Dr. Mendel appeared to recover her senses as she gave him a frosty stare. "As you can see, the automaton had a dangerous malfunction. Surely, even your boss can see I will need to make repairs if I am to complete my job and do a demonstration again."

"He's your boss, too," spat the scrawny man. He appeared to be made entirely of lanky arms and legs. His thin, drawn face was etched with a permanent sneer.

"No, he isn't. I merely have a contract with his

company." Dr. Mendel turned her attention back to Rosie and Lucille.

Rosie had been watching the interaction with her mouth agape. She quickly closed her mouth when she found herself under the scrutiny of the doctor.

"You two are with me."

Rosie's shoulders tensed. She hadn't forgotten the doctor's first instinct was to save her invention over the people on stage.

"I need to get Adam back to the lab." Dr. Mendel's gaze darted from Lucille's still-exposed wrists to Rosie.

Lucille, catching the doctor's look, fumbled to pull down her sleeves.

"What's going on?" asked George. He puffed on his cigar in short, angry bursts.

"Nothing that's any of your concern," Dr. Mendel grunted as she lifted Adam from his propped-up position. "Can you two help me with this? I have a charging station back at my lab."

Rosie exchanged an uneasy glance with Lucille. She wanted to flee, but she was curious about why the doctor wasn't saying anything about Lucille's arms.

Lucille shrugged, answering Rosie's silent question.

Rosie nodded her head. "Lead the way."

As they were leaving, steam hissed out of one of Lucille's compressors.

"What was that?" Rosie heard George ask.

Luckily, the fire brigade chose that moment to cut the power. In the darkened hall, the sound of their steam-powered hoses drowned out any other inquiries from the henchmen.

"Just keep moving, ladies. I'll explain back at the lab," Dr. Mendel whispered.

At last, they reached Dr. Mendel's quarters, in a tiny village of hastily constructed shacks spread out over a clearing on the edge of the exposition grounds. After the doctor ushered them inside, she closed the door with a loud thud, causing Rosie and Lucille to jump.

"I'm sorry." Dr. Mendel's shoulders slumped. "I'm furious they showed up to harass me again."

"I'm just glad we're all safe," Rosie answered. "How's your automaton?"

Dr. Mendel pointed to the raised table in the center of the room. "Would you please lay Adam on the table?" she asked Lucille. "This outfit is only for show, I'm afraid. I need to change before I work on him."

The doctor clicked her tongue as she examined her dress. "Although there's no saving this gown. I've singed the hemline."

Wordlessly, Lucille laid the automaton down while Rosie stared after Dr. Mendel as she disappeared behind a changing screen next to a large open steamer trunk, propped up to be a traveling wardrobe.

With nothing else to do while they waited, Rosie studied the curious shack. It was as if someone had combined a cozy cottage with a laboratory. Near the front door there was a kitchenette with floral dishes stacked neatly next to spare gears. In the center of the shack was the sitting room with a raised table as the focal point. A sofa and two overstuffed armchairs flanked it for snug seating. At the back of the room was the dressing area, along with a curtained off section. Rosie presumed the doctor's sleeping quarters were behind it.

Dr. Mendel emerged from behind the screen, wearing a more practical trousers and button-up shirt combination.

"Much better," she beamed, making her way to the table. The doctor reached behind the automaton's left ear, flicking a switch.

A gentle humming noise emitted from the automaton. The machine's eyes flickered to life, glowing with a steady white light. "What happened?"

"Your safety switch kicked in when you got angry with some hecklers at the demonstration. You accidentally set the stage on fire. Are you damaged?" Dr. Mendel studied her work carefully.

"My systems appear to be intact." Adam flexed his mechanical hands.

"Wonderful!"

To Rosie and Lucille, Dr. Mendel explained, "His safety switch caused the crash. It still needs refinement." She shook her head. "I must sort that out before our next appearance."

"Why exactly does he need a safety switch?" Rosie asked, taking a small step back.

Dr. Mendel shook her head. "It's one of the first things Adam asked for when he started talking."

"I do not wish to lose control. My body is powerful. I don't want to cause harm." Adam stretched as he got down and sat on the sofa.

Rosie blinked. "What?" She retreated to the kitchenette to stand by Lucille, keeping her eyes on Adam.

"It's a lengthy tale." Dr. Mendel brushed off a speck of debris off the table.

Lucille's brows furrowed as she leaned against the counter. She studied Adam, her expression inscrutable.

Rosie was torn. She wanted to ask more about the switch and the men who showed up with the fire brigade, but she also wanted to go back to enjoying the Fair. She was over life and death adventures, and this was sounding like the beginning of another.

"Right. If that's everything, we'll be going."

Lucille looked back uncertainly at Dr. Mendel, but nodded.

Dr. Mendel narrowed her eyes. "Why did your friend have compressors going off every few feet when we were walking here? And don't think I didn't notice her mechanical wrists."

The color on Lucille's ashen face drained.

"Good day." Rosie tugged on Lucille as she guided her distressed friend to the door.

"Wait! I'm sorry. I didn't mean any offense. It's none of my business. I thought-" Dr. Mendel shook her head. "Never mind. Stay, have a drink, and I'll tell you my story if you'd like. I find myself constantly on edge these days. I needed to know you weren't spies. And if you're not, I need to warn you to stay clear of Edison's men."

Rosie exchanged an uneasy glance with Lucille, who already had a foot out the door as soon as the doctor mentioned compressors.

"It's up to you," Rosie told her. She wanted to flee, but the warning intrigued her.

Lucille pursed her lips before answering, "We can stay, but if she asks too many questions, we're leaving."

Dr. Mendel reached behind the sofa and pulled out a monogrammed silver flask. She took a long swig before offering it to Rosie and Lucille.

"You can call me Evelyn. Have a drink."

Rosie took a sip and sputtered at the scorching aftertaste. Lucille, upon observing Rosie's reaction, declined.

"Edison's men have been hounding me for days." Evelyn drank deeply from the flask. "Officially, they're here on behalf of General Electric Company. I'm under contract to present under their name. In exchange, they fund my research." She pinched the bridge of her nose.

"The company has no claim to my work or patents. This was supposed to be a bit of entertainment for the masses. Then my R.I.B. technology took off, and now they want to renegotiate." She snorted and took another drink. "I wish I hadn't needed the money. Before this, I was working out of a converted barn on my parents' orchard."

"Rib?" asked Rosie. She settled into the armchair on the sofa's left side, leaning forward.

"Rational Iteration Biometrics. I took Babbage's Analytical Engine idea and improved it." She traced the flask's engraved letters absently. "Actually, that's an understatement. I made it compact, added functionality, and unintentionally made Adam sentient."

"A sentient machine?"

Lucille shrugged. "I've heard of stranger things."

Loud, authoritative knocking interrupted whatever Evelyn was about to say next. Her eyes grew wide.

"Act natural," she hissed.

It was too late for Rosie and Lucille to hide. The light behind Adam's sensors faded as he powered himself down.

Evelyn's showman persona was in full effect. "Mr. Davies, what can I do for you?" Her voice was saccharin.

"Dr. Mendel, you look lovely as ever." The man at the door wore a crisp, white suit and his spectacles had blue-tinted lenses. He pocketed the sun spectacles as he confidently strode inside. "I hope I didn't catch you at an inconvenient time. I have important business to discuss with you."

Rosie couldn't place his accent. It sounded vaguely southern. Maybe Georgian?

Evelyn crossed her arms. "If it's the same business your

associates approached me with earlier, I'm afraid I already gave my answer: no. But please, come in and have a drink."

Mr. Davies' gaze landed on Lucille and Rosie.

Rosie sat with her hands primly in her lap while Lucille sat in the armchair on the other side of the sofa studying an Exposition pamphlet.

"I see you already have company. Please forgive my intrusion."

He turned to Rosie. She felt herself shrinking under the intense scrutiny of his gaze.

"I find myself at a disadvantage," he said. "You are?"

"Honora Quaman," Rosie blurted, silently apologizing to her boss for using her name, but this was an emergency. Her heart thudded. So much for anonymity. She'd be damned if she gave her actual name. She prayed Lucille would catch on.

"A pleasure to meet you, Ms. Quaman." Mr. Davies' voice was smooth like honeyed whiskey. "And you are?" He raised an inquisitive brow at Lucille.

"Katherine St. James," Lucille replied without missing a beat.

The tightness in Rosie's throat loosened. She wouldn't have guessed that her friend was capable of deception.

Mr. Davies made himself comfortable on the sofa. He leaned back casually, crossing one leg over the other. Rosie stared at his snake-skin boots.

He caught Rosie's gaze and smirked. "They're the most comfortable pair of boots I own."

"Oh." Rosie didn't know what to say to that. Her skin prickled from the heat. Sweat droplets pooled on the back of her neck, soaking the bottom of her red headscarf.

Evelyn spared Rosie any more verbal fumbling by handing Mr. Davies a glass of water. "Here you go," she said. "Can I get either of you a refill?" she asked Rosie and Lucille.

"No, thank you," Rosie replied.

Lucille shook her head no.

Evelyn took a sip from her flask after sitting down on the other side of the sofa, putting herself between Mr. Davies and Lucille.

The tension between Rosie's shoulder blades subsided a fraction. The less Mr. Davies paid attention to Lucille, the better.

"What brings you here, Mr. Davies?"

"I'm not sure I should discuss this in front of your guests." He gave Lucille and Rosie a dubious look.

"Whatever you have to discuss with me, you can discuss in front of them."

"I'm sorry. Who are they to you?" Mr. Davies' brows furrowed.

Evelyn sniffed. "I'm sure it's none of your concern, Mr. Davies, but they're old friends, here to visit the Exposition."

Rosie tried to not look surprised. She resisted the urge to fidget in her seat. Instead, she focused on the weight of her hands resting on her lap.

Mr. Davies turned his attention to Evelyn.

"I heard from the boys you didn't accept our generous offer." Mr. Davies steepled his fingers.

"The brutes who demanded Adam on the spot?" Evelyn snorted. "I'll have you know I'm still contracted to demonstrate with him. I can't hand him off. There are no spares. It would be impossible to do The Living Metal Man show without its namesake."

Mr. Davies inclined his head. "I beg your pardon, Dr. Mendel, but did you refer to the automaton as 'him?' That's fascinating."

Evelyn flushed. "Sorry. I'm used to doing so for the show."

"I see."

Though Rosie wasn't in the direct line of fire of his unblinking stare, she squirmed in her seat.

Mr. Davies stood up and paced. "I'm here on behalf of General Electric Company. Your contract is generous, Dr. Mendel. You have free rein for the duration of the World's Fair." He paused for a sip of water. "However, there is an option in the contract for the company to buy out your patents if it proves to be a lucrative idea. What you've created with Adam is astonishing. Mr. Edison is personally interested in your work."

Evelyn sat her flask down. "I'm flattered, but as I've told your men, I don't see how Adam could be profitable for the company."

"Are you familiar with Krupp's baby?" Mr. Davies leaned toward Evelyn conspiratorially.

"You mean Krupp's pet monster? Who at the Exposition hasn't heard about it?" Evelyn slid closer to Lucille.

Rosie suppressed a shiver. She and Lucille didn't stay long at the Krupp Pavilion. The weapons baron had gone all out for his gun display as the main attraction of the collection boasted to be the world's largest cannon, capable of firing a 2,000-pound projectile for miles. The exhibit made her feel queasy. Lucille didn't protest when she asked to leave.

"Yes, well, you might not be aware of this, but Mr. Edison is understandably concerned about the consequences of a foreign power holding such technology. He believes our own military should prepare for anything. A battalion of automatons might be the creative edge America needs to protect her interests."

Rosie's blood froze.

"Automatons are expensive to build and have limits." Evelyn shook her head. "I've given my answer. I need to repair Adam before the next demonstration. Before your men barged in, Adam had a glitch during the show. The fire brigade was summoned. I need to repair it before tomorrow, or the show won't go on. If I even still have a stage after the accident."

"Yes, but-"

Sparks flying from the automaton resting in his charging station interrupted Mr. Davies.

"Oh, no! There it goes again." Evelyn flew across the room to inspect Adam. "I'm sorry, but I need to cut this short. Good day to you."

Mr. Davies frowned and donned his hat. "This isn't the last you've heard from me, Dr. Mendel. Good day to you."

He slammed the door when he departed, rattling the shack.

"Excellent work, Adam." Evelyn unplugged the automaton from the charging station. "Are you sure you didn't hurt yourself? The sparking was convincing."

"I am fine." His monotone voice sounded petulant. "Did the man go away?"

"For now, yes." Evelyn sighed. "He said he'd be back."

"I do not look forward to his return." Adam's motors buzzed angrily.

"Me, neither."

Rosie let out a breath she didn't realize she was holding.

Evelyn startled, as if she had forgotten Rosie and Lucille were there. "I'm sorry. I didn't mean to involve you both with this business."

"It happens."

"What are you going to do?" asked Lucille. She fixed her gaze on Evelyn and Adam.

Evelyn's shoulders slumped. "I don't know." She ran her hand through her hair, shaking more blond strands free from her wilting up-do. "I'm tempted to pack up Adam now and send him away, out of reach from the company. I don't even know where I could safely send him. Until Mr. Davies' visit, I couldn't have imagined why the sudden interest in my work when all their correspondence had referred to it as sideshow fodder."

Adam walked over to Mr. Davies' vacated seat and sat down, holding his face in his hands.

Rosie spoke before she could consider her words. "I work for the railway. I'm only a fireman, but I could get him in the baggage car with no questions asked."

Evelyn's eyes widened. "That would be wonderful, but where could he go?" She hesitated, before adding, "I developed an artificial skin for Adam to help him blend in crowds. It would help divert attention away from him to at least escape. But he's not interested in using it."

"You have... artificial skin?" Rosie straightened in her seat.

Evelyn nodded. "Before I switched my focus to engineering, I attended medical school. My goal has always been to use science for the betterment of humanity."

She crossed the room to a cheerful painting of an English garden. "I created the skin long before I thought about building an automaton. My uncle was burned severely in a factory accident years ago. He was self-conscious until the day he died about the scarring."

She removed the painting from the wall, revealing a built-in safe. From the safe, she withdrew a briefcase and placed it gently on the elevated table. "It was a pity nothing could be done for him. I have plans to make this accessible for hospitals after I'm done experimenting with the polyvinyl chloride."

She unlocked the case and inside were rows of smooth, artificial skin in various hues.

Lucille's face lit up.

"If Adam would use it, we could walk him off the grounds, with no one being the wiser. No one else knows this."

Adam lifted his head up and faced Evelyn. "No."

"What do you mean?" The doctor met his gaze.

"I do not wish to be human." His internal mechanisms buzzed. "I do not wish to assimilate. My small glimpse of humanity has been enough. Please don't make me." He crossed his arms and rocked back and forth slightly.

"You don't have to do it," Evelyn patted his arm. "I only suggested it so we could sneak you off the grounds. What do you want to do?"

"What do I want?" Adam's modulated voice sounded choked up. "I only want to be me. I want to exist."

Evelyn clicked her tongue. "I want you to exist, too. That's why we need a plan, before Edison's men are back. Do you have any suggestions?"

"No. I do not know what I am. I'm the first of my kind, and perhaps I may end up being the only one. I hope to find out what it means to be me." Adam looked down and his shoulders slumped.

"We'll figure out something." Evelyn hesitated, then asked, "What would help you discover who you are?"

"Your family's orchard sounds beautiful. I would love to learn how to grow things. Maybe I could be of help?"

Evelyn blinked. "I suppose Mother and Father wouldn't mind if I explain the situation to them." She scratched the back of her neck. "That'll be one hell of a telegram."

"Will you come, too?" Adam's eyes shone with soft light.

Evelyn blanched, but recovered quickly. "I suppose I must. Once you're gone, it's not like the company will let me walk free. I'll have to meet up with you later, though. If I leave too soon, it'll look suspicious."

Rosie hit the table excitedly, causing everyone else to stare at her. "I've got it! We'll fake Adam's escape, then hide some of his parts near a river. Make it look like he didn't get far."

"That could work. We have plenty of spare parts. What do you think?" he asked Evelyn.

"It's a sound plan, but why risk helping us?" Doubt clouded Evelyn's face.

"Because, well…" Rosie stammered. She hated being put on the spot. "It's the right thing to do."

Evelyn looked nonplussed.

Lucille tapped Evelyn's shoulder. "This is why." She removed her gloves and pushed up her sleeves. Her mechanical arms and hydraulic hoses, filled with blackish-red fluid, were fully exposed.

Rosie and Evelyn both clamped their hands over their mouths, though Rosie suspected for entirely different reasons. She wanted to ask Lucille if she had lost all sense of self-preservation.

"Are you an automaton, too? But you're so lifelike! A little scarred, but still…" Her voice trailed off as she gaped at Lucille.

"No, I'm something else entirely." Lucille donned her gloves and fixed her sleeves. "What I will tell you is Rosie is the most selfless person I've met."

Hot tears pricked in Rosie's eyes. She furtively dabbed her eyes with her handkerchief.

"Also," Lucille added, "I want some skin."

Evelyn was convinced. She nodded and turned to Rosie. "When does your train leave?"

Rosie retrieved her logbook and flipped it to a page full of timetables. "8:00 am. I report to the station before dawn to prepare the engine, though."

Evelyn nodded. "We can't plant the evidence too soon. I'll place the parts if I can leave Adam with you first." She looked at the automaton. "Would that be all right with you? I'd need to pack you in a trunk to avoid detection."

"It's the most logical choice. I consent to the temporary stasis."

"Are you worried about the journey?"

Adam sat quietly for a moment. "No. I trust you."

Evelyn blinked back tears. "We can make this work. I'll continue my research from the farm, at least until we can figure out something more permanent. It's a quick train ride to New York City if I need supplies."

Rosie felt a tug on her heartstrings. "My route goes to Pittsburgh. It won't get you all the way where you need to go, but I'll help you with the first leg of your journey."

"Thank you. I know we could use all the help we can get."

"I'll leave our address for you." Rosie ripped a page out of her logbook and scribbled the hotel's address on it. Lucille stared at the artificial skin with longing.

"Do you have time to install the skin before we go?" Rosie asked as she handed the address to Evelyn. "The hoses on her limbs are completely exposed underneath her clothes. They need better protection."

"Rosie!" Lucille looked mortified.

"Well, it's true!"

"Of course, of course! It's the least I can do after everything you've done for us." Evelyn stood. "Let me fetch my tools."

"You're welcome," Rosie ribbed Lucille.

"You're incorrigible." Lucille muttered.

Rosie sobered. "I'm sorry if I overstepped my bounds. I didn't mean to embarrass you."

Lucille shrugged, then gave Rosie a shy smile. "It's okay. And thank you. It'll be good to have the hoses covered up. Less nerve-wracking getting dressed every day."

Rosie beamed.

Lucille was pensive on the way out of Evelyn's lab. She rotated her arm in front of her, watching the light catch on the artificial skin a few shades ruddier than her own.

"What's on your mind?" Rosie asked.

"I can't help but wonder if my life would be like Adam's if I hadn't escaped Dr. Prendergast." Lucille dropped her arm and gazed into the distance.

Rosie guided her away from walking into a lovely display of botanicals. "She didn't strike me as one for the spotlight. She seemed more likely to perform increasingly awful experiments on you in the name of progress."

Lucille snorted. "True, but she would talk about investors and proving them wrong. I don't know who she was talking about specifically, though. Who would invest in something like me?" She gestured to herself in distaste.

Rosie took Lucille by the elbow before her friend could draw more attention to herself. Passersby strolled along the path, admiring the vistas. Lucille must have realized what she was doing, because she relaxed and fell into step with Rosie.

"I'm not sure who would invest in technology like you," Rosie muttered only loud enough for Lucille's ears, "But we can't be too careful. Whoever they are, they can't have too many scruples."

"Yes, you're right." Lucille mused. Her expression was pensive as she lapsed back into silence.

Rosie had to save her from walking headlong into a garbage bin. As she righted Lucille, she asked, "That isn't the only thing on your mind, is it?"

Lucille shook her head and let out a sigh. "You go back to work soon, and I don't know what I should do next."

Rosie frowned. "My offer still stands. You can stay at my apartment until you figure it out. There's no rush, is there?"

"No, I suppose not." Lucille's face fell. "I'm afraid the longer I stay with you, the more endangered you'll be."

Rosie squeezed her friend's hand, marveling at how life-life the artificial skin felt. "Hey, we've covered this already. You said yourself that we'll be fine. Remember?"

Lucille's smile was weak. "I know. I don't want to be a burden. That's all."

"You're not. Let's enjoy our last hours while we're here." Rosie scrunched her face. "I don't even want to think about shoveling coal right now. My arms are sore at the mention of it."

"I thought you were sore from the fighting yesterday," Lucille said dryly as they continued along the thoroughfare.

"Let's try to salvage the rest of the day and head back." Rosie sighed. "Tomorrow will be a long day."

Rosie awoke from a deep, restful sleep to frantic pounding on the door and Lucille's mechanical legs bumping into the sparse furniture of the hotel room.

"Oof!" Lucille's foot caught on the corner of Rosie's bed. She teetered precariously.

"What's going on?" Rosie croaked. She rubbed sleep from her eyes and frowned at Lucille.

"Don't know. Trying to get to the door," Lucille grunted, kicking off the bed skirt trapping her leg.

"They've taken Adam!" Evelyn's muffled voice was punctuated by knocking.

"Keep it down!" a neighboring guest shouted.

Rosie dashed out of bed, careful to not bump into Lucille as she freed herself.

She opened the door to a disheveled Evelyn in a dressing gown, clutching a beaded bag.

Rosie turned on the gas lamps.

"They broke in and took him, charging station and all," Evelyn said after Rosie closed the door. "I couldn't fight them off."

In the dim lighting, Rosie could make out scrapes and bruises blooming across Evelyn's jaw.

Rosie clenched her fist.

"Any idea where they took him?"

Evelyn threw her hands in the air and paced. "For all I know, they have him on a train now." Her eyes widened. "But Mr. Davies has an office here in the city."

"Do you have the address?" Lucille prompted.

"Yes! I have his card here." Evelyn retrieved a business card from her small bag. She held up a crisp card with "General Electric Company Chicago Office" underneath Mr. Davies' name typed neatly.

"Let's find you some clothes and go!" Rosie sprang into action, digging through her trunk stashed under the bed.

Tears filled the corners of Evelyn's eyes. "Thank you. I didn't know where to turn."

"We'll do our best to find him. No one in their right mind wants an automaton army." Rosie handed Evelyn spare coveralls and a shirt. "It'll be a little short on you, but it'll keep your modesty intact and give you more freedom of movement than your dressing gown."

Evelyn answered her with a watery chuckle. "I appreciate it."

Rosie was thankful for a cloudless night. The gas lamps illuminated the city streets, but they couldn't keep all the shadows at bay. During daylight hours, the skyscrapers had impressed her, but now, as the midnight hour drew near, their presence felt looming and oppressive. She shivered, despite the muggy air.

Several blocks and wrong turns later, they arrived at the address on Mr. Davies' card. The three women huddled together, looking at the card and the massive building in front of them near the river docks. It looked to be less of an office and more of a warehouse.

"Is this right?" Evelyn asked, creases forming a deep frown on her face.

"It looks suspicious enough," muttered Rosie. A breeze wafted the stench of the polluted river towards them. She gagged. "No wonder it's deserted. The smell alone is enough of a deterrent."

"Are we still going in?" Lucille eyed the building. She set down her lantern to roll her shoulders. "I don't like how close it is to the water."

"We have no choice." Rosie turned to Lucille. "Do you want to stay behind? If you fell into their hands, there's no telling what they might do to you."

Lucille shook her head. "I'll be fine. If there's a chance

Adam's in there, you two wouldn't be able to lift him alone."

"Fair," Rosie conceded, knowing she was right. "But if it looks like we'll be caught, please get yourself out of there."

"I'll be careful." Lucille tentatively brushed Rosie's furrowed brow. "I promise."

"Ready?" Evelyn asked. She had Rosie's borrowed cutters in hand, poised to break the chained padlock on the gate outside the warehouse.

"As we'll ever be." Rosie nodded, doing her best to ignore the butterflies in her stomach.

Evelyn snapped the chain.

Rosie and Lucille dove for the lock a moment too late, and they all held their breath as the broken chain clanked against the gate.

No one raised an alarm. Were there no guards patrolling the warehouse perimeter?

Rosie pushed the gate. It opened with a slow squeak. With growing trepidation, she entered the building with the others following behind her.

Lucille shone her lantern inside the warehouse. It looked as Rosie expected. Shipping crates were stacked neatly, all bearing "General Electric Company" on the sides.

"We're too late," Evelyn whispered. Her voice shook, choking back tears.

"I don't think so." Rosie said, tapping Evelyn and Lucille's arms. "Listen."

Lucille dimmed her lantern as Mr. Davies' cronies appeared ahead, arguing on the other side of a haphazard stack of crates.

"Why's it so quiet? I don't like it, George," the scrawny one said, scratching his neck.

"Mr. Davies said it needs guarded. I've got the seniority, so you're staying." George replied.

"I'm not guarding it!"

"Oh, yes, you are!"

A scuffle broke out. The men crashed into boxes and swore epithets even Rosie was unfamiliar with. She'd have to update Honora tomorrow.

"Now what?" Lucille grumbled.

"Let's find Adam," Rosie muttered. "Sounds like he's here somewhere. And with those two fighting, we can catch them by surprise."

Lucille nodded at the crates next to the henchmen. "I could knock those on them if it comes down to it."

"I'll go with Evelyn, then. Be careful." To the doctor, Rosie asked, "Ready?"

The blood had drained from Evelyn's face. In the dim moonlight streaming through the ceiling windows, she looked like a wild-eyed apparition, as ashen as Lucille. Biting her lip, she nodded. They crept around the crates as the two men brawled.

They found Adam close by, inexpertly bound to his charging station with fraying rope. The gleam of light in his eye sensors was gone and his head drooped.

Rosie shot a worried look at Evelyn, but the doctor didn't seem concerned. She was struggling to untie the rope by hand. Rosie flicked open her pocket knife and motioned the doctor back. Just as she made headway sawing through the rope, Evelyn hissed, "Hurry!"

The men had noticed Evelyn and Rosie's presence.

"What are you doing here?" snarled George at Evelyn. "I told you to stay put!"

Evelyn stammered as Lucille shoved the stacked crates

on the men. The cargo crashed into them, and they heard screams and groans of pain as the rubble settled. Rosie cut the last strands of rope.

"Adam." Evelyn checked him over, biting her lip. "Wake up. You're safe." She paused, then spun to Rosie with an outstretched hand, as if expecting her to produce a toolkit. "Something's wrong with his safety switch."

"You can fix it later. Lucille? A little help here!"

They both looked to where Lucille emerged, hands raised.

"We have a problem," Lucille's voice was strained. She was prodded around the fallen crates, held at gunpoint by Mr. Davies. He smiled.

"I knew you would cause trouble, Dr. Mendel. I didn't expect you to bring me such interesting friends, though."

Rosie's stomach roiled.

"Adam, now would be a marvelous time to wake up." Evelyn pleaded, shaking him by the shoulders. "Please!"

Mr. Davies cast a disapproving glance at his henchmen, still moaning beneath the pile of fallen crates. "What's the point in delegating when you cause me more work?" He clicked the safety on the revolver and dug it further into Lucille's side. "What I need is better help."

Rosie's nails bit into her palms, her pocket knife uselessly clenched in her fist.

"Now, here's what will happen." Mr. Davies sneered. "You three will wait in my office until the freight comes for the automaton. Once it's loaded, I'll decide if I'm turning you over to the authorities. They'll be interested in this one." He tapped the muzzle of the revolver on Lucille's shoulder thoughtfully. She flinched. "I've seen nothing like it before."

Evelyn stepped forward, palms outstretched. "Please, don't do this. They were only here to help me."

"Then I'm sure we can come to an amicable agreement." His grin widened.

Rosie glanced down and reached the few inches to Adam's safety switch. It was jammed and blocking a critical part of his circuitry. It would be impossible to fix here. But.

Rosie's pulse raced as she shuffled closer, the blood rushing in her ears, drowning out whatever Mr. Davies and Evelyn were saying. Gritting her teeth, she angled the blade of her pocket knife like a lever, and ripped the safety switch off. Hopefully, Adam would still recognize her as friendly.

"Help us," she hissed, then dodged from his line of sight.

Adam's system crackled to life. His eye sensors flashed green as his head snapped toward Evelyn. The automaton rocked forward and charged.

"Adam!" Evelyn cried as the automaton planted himself in front of her, facing Mr. Davies with his arms outstretched.

"I abhor violence, but I will snap your neck if you harm her." The air around the automaton sparked, smelling of burnt ozone.

Mr. Davies' eyes went wide, and he swung the revolver from Lucille to Adam. A shot rang out, tearing a hole through a crate.

Seizing the moment, Lucille balled her fists together and struck the side of Mr. Davies' temple with a hammer blow. Her compressors steamed and hissed at the impact. He fell, the revolver skidding out of his hand.

Rosie stepped over and carefully picked up the dropped

revolver. It felt clunky and foreign in her hand. She willed her grip to remain steady and marched to the fallen henchmen. Flanked by Adam and Lucille, she drew the gun on George as he struggled to shift the broken crates off him.

"We're leaving. Don't follow."

George's scoff was pained. "Go wherever you like. Just take the damn machine with you. It's more trouble than it's worth."

The other henchman groaned in response.

"It's 'he', but thank you." Evelyn appeared on Adam's left. "Mr. Davies is alive, but I made sure he won't be bothering us if he wakes up soon."

"Great," Lucille said. "Let's get the hell out of here."

Outside, Rosie chucked the revolver in the river. Lucille raised her brows.

Rosie shrugged. "I don't want it."

"I can't say I'm sad to see it go."

"We still have a problem," Evelyn piped up. "What am I going to do with Adam now? Mr. Davies won't forget this."

"I have an idea," Rosie replied.

Back at Evelyn's shack, the group packed the doctor and Adam's essentials in trunks, ready to be taken to Lucille and Rosie's hotel room until they could leave the city.

Evelyn scattered the broken remains of Adam's old prototype parts across the lab. It was a gruesome sight. Adam quietly touched his repaired arm as he watched Evelyn toss the last bits.

"Do I have any spare parts left?" he hummed.

"Of course, you do." Evelyn paused and regarded the automaton. "Are you trying to make a joke?"

"Yes. Did I do it correctly?"

Evelyn snorted. "Yes. Here, help break up these old leg pieces."

"With pleasure."

"Do you think they'll be okay?" Lucille asked, somewhere between horrified and fascinated as she watched them strew Adam's parts across the lab.

"I think so." To Evelyn, Rosie asked, "Do you have the hand pieces ready for me?"

Evelyn tossed her two prototypes of Adam's hands. "Here you go."

"I'll get this ready. You might want to leave while I finish this up."

"Thank you."

"Yes, thank you." Adam's eyes were still green. Rosie wondered what other features were unlocked by removing the safety switch. So far, he seemed to be happier.

Lucille helped Evelyn and Adam carry the luggage out of the shack as Rosie turned her attention to the matches and the spare mechanical arm. "Right. Building a fire-starting machine. Should be a breeze," she muttered to herself.

Taking a battery, compressor, and a few other odds and ends, Rosie rigged up a crude motor with an apparatus to attach the hands. She adjusted the grip of one metal hand to turn a gas lamp valve. Rosie lit several candles throughout the shack, then placed a lit match in the other hand. She connected the last wire. The device rotated slowly.

Rosie ran outside.

"Keep your distance!" she panted when she saw the others lingering too close to the shack, Lucille's lantern raised. "I'll catch up with you all at the hotel. I need to make sure this works."

Evelyn nodded as they hurried away. Adam was already packed away in the oversized steamer trunk that Lucille dragged behind her.

Rosie peeked from behind a sturdy tree across from the shack. She was thankful the shacks were so far from the other buildings. She didn't want to burn down the whole fair, but this needed to be thorough.

A thunderous explosion confirmed her crude pyrotechnic machine worked. The rallying cries of the fire brigade echoed throughout the fairgrounds as Rosie made her escape.

Rosie's boss nearly wept when she asked about new openings for an apprentice. The usual brake-van operator was complaining of an injured back and needed help. When Rosie came back with the news, Lucille lit up.

"But are you sure you don't want to go with them?" Rosie asked. "Evelyn could probably figure out a better solution for your limbs than I can."

Lucille shook her head. "I feel safer with you."

"But what about your blood?" Rosie finished doing up her coveralls for their upcoming shift and watched as Lucille stepped into hers.

"What about it?"

Rosie checked her logbook notes for the hundredth time. "I know nothing about its chemistry or how it's made. Just the look and feel and smell. What if you run out?"

"Maybe something will come back to me about it. Or perhaps my borrowed second chance will end. I'd rather use the time I have now wisely." Lucille grasped for the sleeves that dangled awkwardly behind her.

"Yes, but working for the railway?" Rosie grabbed the shoulders of Lucille's coveralls and held them up so she could slide in easier. "And brakeman is one of the most dangerous jobs!"

Lucille shrugged. "It's good enough for you, isn't it? Besides, at least we go on adventures."

Rosie sighed and made for the door. "Okay. I'll see you at the next station after I send in Evelyn's resignation telegram for her. It will be fun concocting a story about poor Adam going mad because of Edison's men." She smiled, but it faded as Lucille finished buttoning herself up. "Please be safe."

"I will." Lucille rolled up her sleeves, double-checking the artificial skin was in place. As long as no one questioned its sheen, she would be fine. She looked up sharply. "I won't be working with the same conductor I knocked out last time, right?"

Rosie shook her head and laughed. "No, it's not him today."

Lucille readjusted her sleeves. "Thank goodness."

"Good luck." Rosie hesitated in the doorway. "If anyone gives you problems, let me know."

Lucille's eye crinkles as she gave her a warm smile. "I will."

"How was the Fair?" Honora asked, startling Rosie. She had been diligently feeding the firebox, wanting to put as much distance between the train and Chicago as possible. The shovelful of coal scattered on the floor.

"I'm sorry, what?" Rosie scrambled to scoop up the coal.

Honora guffawed. "I asked how the Fair was. Did it meet your expectations?"

"It was…" Rosie struggled to find the words. After the last few days, her emotions were running high. "Extraordinary. But I think I'm ready to get back to normal."

"Really?" Honora scoffed. "That's too bad. I heard there's going to be some big electrical conference later this summer there. Your hero's rumored to be giving a lecture."

"Nikola Tesla?" Rosie shot up, bumping her head on a valve. Cursing, she rubbed her head with soot-covered hands as Honora tsked and shouldered her out of the way.

"Is that his name?" the engineer deadpanned as she adjusted the boiler panel. "I'd forgotten."

"Well, maybe I'll be ready for a break by then. There's all those unfinished exhibits, too." Rosie mused.

The conductor took the ticket from the woman's slender hands. Her pinned up dyed hair had a lone white streak in it.

"There you go, ma'am. I hope you have an enjoyable trip."

"Thank you," she replied as she stepped aboard the train. "But it's 'doctor.'" The soft morning light reflected off her half-moon spectacles as she went to her seat.

THE ASSISTANT

Last time, Rosie and Lucille helped the automaton, Adam, and his creator, Dr. Evelyn Mendel, escape the clutches of Edison's men. Unbeknownst to our heroines, a sinister familiar face threatens their newfound peace. To understand what happens next, first let's travel back to 1871, to the St. James' Orphan Asylum for Girls.

I should have calmed down before I picked up the ax. I brought it down, and the impact jarred my entire body. My teeth clenched, and I bit my tongue. The ax stuck in the stump; the log remained upright and intact. I let out a string of curses that would have earned me floor scrubbing duty and three Hail Marys if any of the nuns had been in earshot. As it was, the nuns were the source of my ire. For once in my nearly eighteen years, I didn't care who heard me.

I kept up the swearing as a litany as I gripped the ax's handle and made my stance wide. My too-small, secondhand boots pinched as I adjusted my stance for the optimum angle for leverage. Sweat beaded on my forehead. Summer was lingering this year, but the trees would change colors soon. Gritting my teeth, I prepared to swing again. I was furious, but I'd be damned if the orphanage didn't have enough firewood before the chill set in.

Before I could swing again, a small voice behind me called out, "Constance? Are you okay?"

I carefully placed the ax next to the stump, then turned. A little girl named Lucille stood clutching an intricate doll. The almost six-year-old had only been at the orphanage for a few weeks. Warm sunlight gave her a halo reflected in her golden hair. Bits of jam clinging to her second-or-third-hand, oversized dress, plus the mud near its hem, spoiled the cherubic effect.

"I'm fine. My ax missed, that's all." I didn't want to add to Lucille's worries. She was having a hard time adjusting to orphanage life. The nuns said the rest of her family perished in a fire. She was the sole survivor. Even the house was reduced to ash and rubble.

I couldn't imagine the pain she must have felt. The nuns found me as an infant on the steps of the orphanage in a basket with dirty swaddling and a hastily scribbled note with my name on it. A dusting of snow obscured any evidence of whoever left me out in the cold without at least knocking. They guessed I was about three months old, so they chose October 1st to mark my birthday.

No one ever came to claim me.

"Are you sure?" Lucille's guileless eyes were wide as she peered up at me.

"I'm fine." I wiped the sweat off my forehead with my handkerchief and pocketed it. "What's wrong with your doll?"

Tears filled her eyes. "Marybeth won't plié anymore. Can you fix her?"

"Let me look." Lucille put the delicate doll in my waiting palm. I was careful to not crumple the toy's gauzy white tutu. Closer inspection revealed some jam from Lucille's hand had migrated to the winder on the back of the doll, enough to prevent it from being turned. I untucked a bit of my shirt from my trousers and used the tail of it to wipe off the worst of the debris. I scraped away the last stubborn bits with my nails. After nudging a gear back into place on the doll's back, I turned the winder experimentally. A soft music box tune emitted from the doll as it sank into a slow plié.

"There you go. Next time, wash up after breakfast, okay?" I smiled, hoping Lucille wouldn't take it badly. Goodness knows some nuns here could be too strict. She didn't need anyone else telling her what to do.

"I will! Thank you so much!" Lucille beamed and hugged me, burying her face in my stomach. "I'm so happy I have you to talk to. The other kids won't play with me." Her voice was muffled in my sternum. "I don't know what I did wrong."

"You haven't done anything wrong." I ruffled her hair. "It's tough when you're new. Most of the others have been here for a long time."

"Like you?" Lucille looked up at me, her toothy grin meaning well, but my heart shattered.

I'm the orphanage's longest resident. Most of the nuns on staff haven't been here as long as I have.

"Yes. But don't worry. You'll be fine." I patted her shoulder. "Someone will come along and adopt you; I'm sure of it."

"Or I'll stay here with you. We can be best friends forever!"

Lucille's enthusiasm was contagious. I smiled, despite the growing dread in the pit of my stomach.

"Always."

I gestured to the tree stump behind me. "I need to get back to work now, but I'll see you later."

"Can you play after dinner?"

"You've got it."

Lucille scampered away, singing a nursery rhyme without a care in the world.

I couldn't tell her as of earlier this morning that my days left at the orphanage were numbered.

"You wanted to see me?" I asked as I struggled to sit on the child-size stool in Sister Katherine's office. I sat with my ankles crossed, noting I could take the hem out of my new-to-me trousers. When I started doing odd jobs around the orphanage grounds, the nuns allowed me to wear pants. Today they were riding up too high, but I wouldn't be able to take care of it until later. My to-do list today was long, and having to sit in for an unexpected meeting was making me feel antsy. I willed myself to not tap my foot.

"Yes, thank you for coming." Sister Katherine was the youngest nun on staff. She could have been my older sister. I heard a rumor she took her vows because a young man broke her heart, though I found that hard to believe. Most days, Sister Katherine went about her duties with cheerful devotion and a secretive smile.

"Am I in trouble?" I couldn't remember the last time the nuns punished me. I always did my chores without complaining and never ran away, unlike some others. The orphanage was cold and unfeeling, but I was grateful for having a roof over my head. Long ago, I learned to keep my swearing to myself.

"No, not at all." Sister Katherine smiled, but the dark shadows under her bloodshot eyes gave her a haunted look. "It's nearly October. I need to talk to you about your future. Your birthday is fast approaching."

I groaned. "Can't I stay on as a groundskeeper or handyman? I'm already doing the work."

"The orphanage can't afford to hire you. We barely keep everyone fed and clothed," she gently chided.

I hung my head. This was hardly the first time we'd had this conversation. I'd asked before, back when my birthday was still far off, and my future was a hypothetical question. I even had suggested they let me work for room and board, but no one took me seriously.

"I don't know where to go." I chewed my lip. "What if I took my vows and stayed on as a nun?"

"Not knowing what you want isn't a reason to take the vows." Sister Katherine shook her head. "You should experience a bit of the world first. If you feel strongly about it, you can always come back later. You're still young."

I nodded, not meeting her gaze. "If you'll excuse me, I have logs to split." Hot tears prickled at the corners of my eyes. I stumbled standing up from the tiny stool and knocked it over in my haste to leave before I turned a blotchy shade of tomato red, like I always did when I got upset. I could already feel my cheeks burning with unshed tears and anger.

"What's wrong?" Sister Katherine blinked owlishly at me as I righted the stool.

Her tepid concern was too much to bear. Pausing in the doorway, I wished I could tell her what I really thought. "I have work to do. I'll meditate on your words."

The sun was high when I found my rhythm splitting logs. My ax chopped through the wood with a therapeutic whack, echoing along the quaint street. The orphanage was on the outskirts of the city, away from all the bustle. Out here, we still had trees and wildlife, but few pedestrians. When a stranger called out to me between swings, I nearly dropped my ax.

Looking around for the source of the noise, my gaze fell onto a pale woman standing near the property line of the orphanage. She wore all white. The only spot of color on her person was her dark brown hair, pulled back into a severe bun, but even it had a white streak. Her aquiline nose and stern expression made me wonder if she was a visiting nun, though the lack of a habit puzzled me. The sunlight glinted off her spectacles, making her expression unreadable.

I used one hand to shield my eyes.

"Can I help you?"

"That's what I'm wondering." The woman nodded at the enormous pile of lumber I had stacked neatly. "Are you able to do heavy lifting on your own?"

"Yes. All the time." I frowned and scratched the back of my neck with my free hand. "Why do you ask?"

"I need an assistant." She adjusted her spectacles. "Are you reasonably intelligent?"

A creeping blush rose from my collarbone to my face. Sweat and dirt were caked onto my skin and clothes. Strands of my stringy hair were plastered to my skin. "I can read, do my arithmetic, and I'm handy. I build toys for the little ones."

The dour woman smiled at me for the first time. "Excellent. You may be exactly what I'm looking for. I'm

Dr. Zona Prendergast. I'm a biomedical engineer. Would you like to come work for me? I'm conducting medical research and it's nearing its last phase."

I stood there, stunned, for several moments. Sister Katherine's words came back to me, unbidden. She told me to see more of the world.

"Why me?"

"Why not you? You're here. You're strong and seem capable. You're an orphan, yes? Soon to age out of the home?"

I nodded, a lump in my throat.

She continued briskly. "I can't imagine you have many options unless you wanted to be a farmhand or work at a factory. A woman of your size and strength could do well at those things, but I suspect you want more."

I gave her a watery smile. "Thank you."

"Don't thank me yet. Let's go make the arrangements with whoever is in charge here. I don't have time to waste."

It was a whirlwind process leaving the orphanage. Sister Katherine took one look at Dr. Prendergast and told me I still had the option of taking my vows.

I furrowed my brows. "Didn't you tell me to see more of the world first?"

Sister Katherine looked between the doctor and me, chewing her lip, but nodded, resigned.

I gathered my things and said awkward goodbyes to the others. When I came downstairs from the cramped dormitory, Lucille was waiting for me by the door. Her red-rimmed eyes were bright with unshed tears, but she still smiled.

"I'm sorry I won't be able to play after dinner." I kneeled down at her level to pat her shoulder.

"It's okay. I'm glad you have a new mommy." Her voice quavered a bit.

I gave her a tight hug. "Well, she's not adopting me. I'll be working for her."

Lucille nodded in understanding. "You'll do great," she said with a confidence I didn't have.

Warmth flooded my chest. "Thank you, dear girl."

"This is for you. It's the last one left!" Lucille pressed a single daisy into my hand.

"Thank you. I'll treasure it." My throat felt tight as I gave her a hug. "I'll write when I can. Keep studying your letters, okay?"

"I promise!" Lucille grinned.

As we left the orphanage, I asked Dr. Prendergast if she would consider adopting Lucille.

"No," she said flatly. At my horrified expression, she added, "I'm an unmarried woman. My laboratory and work are no place for a child. A girl as charming as she will have no trouble finding a home."

Heat rose in my cheeks as I was hyper-aware of my square jaw and towering frame. The fine hairs on my arms and the back of my neck stood on end as I processed what she said about her line of work.

"You will be fine," Dr. Prendergast told me, as if she could read my thoughts. "You'll be the perfect assistant."

Dr. Prendergast's home was in the heart of New York City. Though I had lived on the edge of town until now, I never ventured farther in. Nothing could have prepared me for the onslaught of filth piled high in the streets or the constant cacophony of noise. I shrank back in the carriage as the precariously close traffic overwhelmed me. When the carriage finally came to a stop, I slumped in my seat, completely spent.

Her home was a detached brick townhouse, with an impressive turret jutting out of its pointed roof. Despite its grand appearance, the lot was cramped between the other buildings. A high iron fence with deadly pointed tips surrounded the tiny yard. Hedges grew on the inside of the fence, obscuring the view of passersby. My eyebrows rose when I noticed decorative iron bars barricaded almost every window.

When I asked the doctor about the barred windows as we exited the carriage, she told me she needed the extra security.

"My work draws a lot of attention. These measures will ensure it is protected until I'm ready to share my findings." Dr. Prendergast patted my arm in a surprising display of affection.

Unease gnawed at my stomach, but I nodded anyway. I jumped when the cab driver wordlessly dumped my trunk next to me. The carriage took off at breakneck speed, disappearing around the corner.

"Coming?" Dr. Prendergast stood in front of the massive ornate gate, waiting.

I picked up my trunk and hurried over. I stared at the overcrowded keyring clenched in Dr. Prendergast's hand as she unlocked the gate. What could she possibly need so many keys for? The gate swung open with a grating squeak. After a short walk to the house, Dr. Prendergast unlocked the front door.

I barely glimpsed the somber parlor before the doctor whisked me upstairs to my quarters. I trudged behind her on the narrow staircase, being careful to not bang my trunk on the worn banister. At the top of the twisting stairway, Dr. Prendergast opened the only door on this floor. It appeared we were in the tower.

Butterflies fluttered in my stomach when Dr. Prendergast opened the door. Bits of angel dust danced in the sunbeams over the bare writing desk facing the open window. The bed looked too short for me, but I didn't care. For the first time, I would have my own room. I wouldn't have to listen to the other girls' snoring all night long.

I turned to express my gratitude to Dr. Prendergast. She looked uncomfortable in the doorway, one foot already out in the hall.

"Thank you so much for everything! This is perfect." Her hunched shoulders stopped me from giving her a hug, but I couldn't help the grin plastered on my face. Even though she wouldn't be a motherly figure for me, she was giving me a place to call home.

The doctor cleared her throat. "I'm glad the room is to your satisfaction. I telegrammed the housekeeper ahead of time so she could air out the spare room before your arrival." Her eyes darted to the desk. "I'll give you some reading material in the morning that will be beneficial for our work. The nun told me you are quite the voracious reader."

I flushed crimson. "Thank you. I won't let you down."

"I'm glad." Dr. Prendergast dropped her gaze to my meager trunk. "I'll let you finish getting settled, then. Dinner is at seven. My housekeeper has taken the rest of the day off for a personal errand. She usually does the cooking." The doctor grimaced. "My culinary skills are lacking, but I should be able to fix us something passable."

I nodded, brimming with excitement.

As she turned to leave, Dr. Prendergast called from the stairwell, "You are free to explore the house, but I caution you to stay out of the lab until I can give you a tour. It's a dangerous place for the uninitiated. Don't go down the elevator without me."

It was only after she left, as I was putting away my few possessions, that I realized she still hadn't told me the nature of her work. What could be so dangerous about medical research?

I woke up at dawn the next day, ready to work.

Unfortunately, I hadn't asked Dr. Prendergast during dinner what time breakfast would be. I had been too busy peppering her with questions about her research, only for her to tell me there would be plenty of time later for that.

Instead, she had wanted to talk about what sort of education the orphanage had given me. She had been disappointed when she found out much of my reading had been of Classical philosophical works. She vowed to fill in the neglected parts of my education. I was puzzled by her reaction, but happy for the attention. Dr. Prendergast's assessment of her own cooking skills had been painfully accurate, but I still scarfed down dinner.

Now, my stomach growled as I opened my bedroom door. I tripped over the stack of books in front of the doorway. Panting, I caught myself before I tumbled down the stairs. My head was inches away from the top of the staircase as I pushed myself off the wood floor. While cleaning up the scattered pile, I found a note on the floor with "Recommended reading" written on it in a spidery script.

After checking that the books were unharmed, I placed them on the writing desk. I flipped through a few out of curiosity. I wasn't familiar with the works of Cornelius Agrippa, Paracelsus, or Albertus Magnus, but I was intrigued by what their works had to do with my new position. My rumbling stomach prevented me from studying them right away.

I ventured down to the dining room, but the house

seemed deserted. I didn't encounter Dr. Prendergast or the housekeeper. Though I had been on a quick tour yesterday, I felt too much like a guest to help myself to the pantry. Dr. Prendergast said I had almost free rein over the house, but wandering around looking for her made me feel uncomfortable for reasons I couldn't quite put my finger on. So, I waited in the dining room for about half an hour before deciding to go back up to my room.

Ignoring my hunger pangs, I threw myself into studying my new reading material. After browsing through the selection, I settled on a book on anatomy. Many of the other books were too arcane for me. I could grasp there was a theme about natural sciences in the recommended reading, but the particulars were lost on me, especially in the ones mentioning alchemy. My thoughts drifted back to the orphanage, and I wondered what Sister Katherine would think of my research.

Finally, a couple of hours later, Dr. Prendergast rapped her knuckles against my open door.

I looked up from my book to see her stifling a yawn and sporting dark circles under her eyes. Otherwise, her appearance was as neat as yesterday, not a single hair out of place from her bun.

"I should have told you to eat without me. My work frequently continues well into the night. I'm a late riser." Despite her efforts, an enormous yawn escaped. She put her hand to her mouth, aghast. "Pardon me. I need coffee now. Breakfast?"

"That would be lovely." My stomach audibly growling ruined my restrained reply.

"Let's go before we further embarrass ourselves."

I thought I saw the flicker of a smile on Dr. Prendergast's face before she went downstairs.

After we ate, Dr. Prendergast took me down the recently installed elevator to the lab in the basement. It was a slow and rickety descent. Its ironwork design made me think of an ornate birdcage. I wished I could have taken the stairs instead, but I wanted to make a good impression on my first full day. When we finally reached the bottom floor, I released my vice-grip on the handrail.

"It's not much further." Dr. Prendergast unlocked a series of padlocks on the heavy wooden door in front of us, partially solving the mystery of why her keyring was so crowded. The door swung open when she finished.

Dr. Prendergast entered the lab first. She pulled a lever on the wall, and soft gas-lamp light illuminated the entire room. Front and center of the room, a row of five skeletons were displayed in various stages of walking. These were no ordinary skeletons. Each one had bones replaced with mechanical parts. Some had artificial arms, others had rebuilt legs. The last one in the row had all of its limbs replaced. It towered over the others. Behind the skeletons, a chalkboard filled with notes, schematics, and equations dominated the wall.

The doctor walked me through the lab in silence as I took in the sights. There were two rows of wooden tables, each with a particular purpose. Stacks of papers with detailed diagrams of various limbs covered one table. Upon closer inspection, I realized some anatomical diagrams were schematics of mechanical limbs. A partially complete silver femur bone laid across the table, next to a complete model of a bony, copper hand.

Separate piles for mold castings of bones and finished metal parts were on the next table. It looked like the doctor was testing out different materials. There were tibiae and fibulae in various types of metals, including iron, copper, silver, gold, and other types I was less familiar with.

One table drew my eye. Half a dozen mechanical hearts made of different metals littered its surface. Spare gears, hoses, and parts I couldn't fathom were strewn over schematics. I wanted to see how it worked. I took a few involuntary steps forward before my eyes landed on a glass display case next to the table. Inside was a set of mechanical lungs suspended from the top of the case. Though the artificial lungs were deflated, the delicate copper and canvas design was beautiful.

"Would you like to see how it works?"

I had all but forgotten Dr. Prendergast's presence. I started at her sudden appearance on my right.

"Yes, please!"

She turned a switch on a compressor at the base of the display case. It wheezed and hissed to life, letting out small puffs of steam. Inside the case, the cloth and copper lungs expanded and contracted. I realized belatedly I was breathing in time with the artificial lungs. I couldn't take my eyes off them.

"It's beautiful," I whispered.

Dr. Prendergast turned off the noisy compressor. "I'm glad you think so. My goal is to give humanity a chance at perfect health. The effects of war, diseases, and industrial accidents will be a thing of the past."

"Incredible." Suddenly, I felt foolish for thinking my bit of studying this morning would prepare me for today. I was out of my depth. "But what do you need me for? It looks like you have everything in hand."

I hated myself for asking, and I dreaded her response. However, I didn't want to be sent away when she inevitably came to the same conclusion later. Better to get this conversation over with now.

The doctor cleared her throat. "My work isn't

complete yet." She pointed to the mechanical heart table. "I've made meaningful strides in all areas of my research, except for this one. I originally intended for you to only help by carrying the heavy equipment. However, the nun said you are mechanically gifted." She peered at me over her half-moon spectacles.

I tinged red. "Well, I built my own toys growing up, then I gifted them to Lucille when she arrived at the orphanage."

Dr. Prendergast blinked, briefly reminding me of Sister Katherine.

Reddening further, I blustered on. "I mean, they were intricate toys. Lots of models and dolls with intricate parts. Her favorite was my old toy ballerina."

"Excellent. Would you be willing to try your hand at the mechanical hearts? I've already finished the theoretical part. I only need the pieces to fit together. It would free my time to focus on a delicate chemistry experiment." She flicked a speck of dust off the nearby table. "It would also allow me to spend more time pursuing funding. Unfortunately, the components I require are costly."

I brightened. "I would love to help!"

I turned my attention to the artificial hearts. I picked up each one gingerly and studied the schematics. Shyly, I asked, "Can I take them apart? It'd help me better understand how it's meant to work."

It surprised me to see Dr. Prendergast was already walking towards a door at the back of the room I hadn't noticed during the tour. Without turning around, she replied, "Yes, please do. How else would you work on it?"

I enthusiastically started taking apart one model, but jumped when the doctor called out, "One last thing: don't come in here. The chemicals are volatile." She closed the backroom door, leaving me to my own devices.

I never met the housekeeper. On my first full day, I had been too excited about getting started that I didn't question where she was at mealtimes. Our food appeared in the dining room like clockwork, and the housework was always finished. It was like living with a benevolent ghost.

After several days into my time at the house, I gathered up the courage to ask Dr. Prendergast about the housekeeper. She easily brushed off my questions, telling me she only worked part time, as the doctor needed most of her money for her research.

"I've also asked her to leave me undisturbed so we may both complete our jobs in peace." Dr. Prendergast tapped her foot. "Is that all you needed?"

"Yes, but," I struggled to put into words why I felt the need to know. Despite finally having a home instead of the orphanage, I felt more isolated than ever. "What's her name?"

Dr. Prendergast frowned. "Why does it matter to you? She does her duty diligently, and I pay her weekly salary. It's been so long I've quite forgotten." At my distraught expression, the doctor hastily amended, "Mrs. Shaloe is her name. See, I remembered. However, I have more pressing matters at hand than socializing with my hired help. Shall we get back to work now?"

I nodded, though I still felt uneasy.

My eighteenth birthday had passed by little fanfare. The doctor presented me with a customized pair of goggles to better see the intricacies of the artificial hearts I worked on. It was more than I expected, and the gesture touched me.

The following months flew by. Most mornings after breakfast, we headed down to the lab. I would work on the mechanical hearts, tinkering away. I loved my job. It reminded me of building toys for Lucille, but with an even greater purpose. We'd break for lunch, though often the doctor would shoo me out of the lab so she could keep working. I wouldn't see the doctor again until our regular tea time, and at dinner. I felt guilty eating my lunch alone, but as much as I wanted to keep working too, I was so tired. No matter how much I slept at night, I never felt fully refreshed in the morning. I was grateful the quality of my craftsmanship never suffered.

We took Sundays off, though I found out quickly the doctor preferred studying to going to mass. I spent my Sundays in my room reading my Bible, saying my prayers, and working through the ever-increasing stack of books the doctor regularly provided me with.

Occasionally, I would write Lucille letters, though I rarely received a response after the first letter I sent. Eventually, the letters stopped coming. I hoped it meant she had been adopted or made friends. My workload and exhaustion prevented me from worrying too much.

Six months in as Dr. Prendergast's assistant, I finished a working mechanical heart. When I presented the completed model to Dr. Prendergast at our daily tea, her lips curved into a wide grin. "It's perfect. I'll bring it to the grant meeting tomorrow."

"You finally have an investor?" My pulse quickened.

She poured my tea, stirred in the sugar, and slid it over to me. "Something like that. I'll be gone most of the day tomorrow, I expect. Why don't you take tomorrow off and rest?"

"You don't want me to come with you?" I was devastated.

"It's not that I don't want you there." Dr. Prendergast pursed her lips. "How do I put this?" She steepled her fingers. "I know how brilliant you are. Never forget that.

But in the eyes of the investors, you are still a child. It would be best for the project if we appear to be as professional as possible."

"I guess."

"I will make sure your name is on the patent paperwork." Dr. Prendergast smiled. "Don't you want what's best for the project?"

"Yes." Hope blossomed in my chest.

"Good girl. Now, drink your tea before it gets cold."

As I sipped my tea, Dr. Prendergast chuckled to herself. It was such an odd thing for her to do that I blurted, "What is it?"

The doctor shook her head, smiling slightly. "I can't believe my good fortune. I finally have a competent assistant. You're the first one to exceed my expectations."

"Oh." I allowed myself a small smile, but I lowered my gaze. I didn't want the doctor to think I was conceited. I went back to drinking my tea until a question gnawed at me. "If you don't mind me asking, what happened to your other assistants?" I absently swirled the cream in my tea.

Dr. Prendergast waved her hand dismissively. "Let me think." She counted off on her fingers, "Eloped, with child, new job, carriage accident, and sanatorium. The latter had a weak constitution, I'm afraid." She took a sip of tea. "I've heard he's made a full-recovery and moved to the country."

"Oh. I'm sorry he had difficulties." I took a drink of my tea, unsure of how else to respond. "That was quite a list."

Dr. Prendergast shook her head. "It sounds much more dramatic than it really was, I assure you. I'm grateful you are made of sterner stuff. But we should let the past rest. We need to prepare for tomorrow."

With that, the conversation was closed, and Dr. Prendergast never mentioned her past assistants again.

The flurry of activity to pack up everything the doctor would need for the meeting lasted late into the night, and I went to bed with aching muscles. I found myself thankful for a day off tomorrow. Maybe I would finally get the rest I needed.

The next day, Dr. Prendergast came home at midmorning. I was reading in the parlor when she opened the door and slammed it shut, rattling the distinguished portraits on the walls. She stormed into the house, throwing the steamer trunk on the floor. I dropped my translated copy of *De Mineralibus* in shock.

"What happened?" I meekly asked, hardly daring to peek at the doctor as I scooped my book.

"What happened? More appropriate to ask what didn't happen," she fumed. She threw off her cloak and paced. She swore several times under her breath before turning to face me. "The board denied us the grant. We have no funding."

"Well, can we go to a bank? Maybe we'd have better luck with a loan?" I kept my tone soft, not wanting to further enrage the doctor. I'd never seen her so angry.

"I highly doubt it." She took a deep breath. "When I told them I needed bodies for test subjects, after the board finished ridiculing my findings, they threatened to summon the constable." Dr. Prendergast shook her head. "I tried to tell them I didn't need live subjects for the heart or lung transplant. We would use cadavers."

My jaw dropped. "What are you talking about? Bodies?"

Dr. Prendergast rolled her eyes. "How on earth did you think we would test out your heart or the lungs? We need subjects. It's no different from what students use at medical schools."

"Yes, I suppose." Doubt crept into my voice. "Why didn't the board see it that way?"

"Because they are small-minded fools," Dr. Prendergast snorted.

The ticking of the cuckoo clock filled the silence between us.

Finally, I asked, "But even if we got the cadavers, how would we know if the heart or lungs worked? They're dead."

Dr. Prendergast's expression flickered with an emotion I couldn't name before she schooled herself to her more stoic appearance. "We'd come up with something. We have to start somewhere. There's always galvanism, I suppose."

I shuddered. I remembered reading about Mr. Galvani's electrical experiments on dead frogs. The illustrations of its twitching legs were grotesque. Of all my readings, his experiments disturbed me the most. I had nightmares for weeks after I first read about them.

"Anyway," the doctor pressed on. "We could always get bodies the way the medical colleges do."

"Buy them?" I asked dubiously.

"Well, yes, or dig them up." Dr. Prendergast shrugged.

The blood drained from my face. I trembled, clenching my fists.

"Never."

Dr. Prendergast sneered. "Really, 'never?' Do you hear yourself, girl? Use your head instead of your heart for once."

"It's morally reprehensible." I threw my hands up in disbelief.

"So is letting humanity continue to suffer. Our work could save so many lives. We only need to test our devices on a few bodies."

I shook my head. "We need to get their families' permission or buy cadavers through the proper channels. We can't let our work become corrupted by our methods."

Dr. Prendergast stared at me. The cuckoo clock announced the top of the hour with a trilling melody. She sighed. "Fine. We'll do it your way. Eventually, you'll see why it won't work."

"It'll work." My voice had more confidence in it than I felt.

"Let's drink some tea and put this fight behind us. Today has been difficult enough." Dr. Prendergast left for the kitchen.

The beginnings of a tension headache spread. I rubbed my temples, wincing.

From the kitchen, the doctor muttered, "You're a fool if you think the universities only use legally obtained bodies."

My heart sank.

The next few weeks were tense. We continued our work in the lab, but Dr. Prendergast was often sullen as she buried herself in her chemistry experiment. Most days she skipped our tea time, and sometimes even missed dinner.

I threw myself into perfecting the mechanical heart. It was ticking flawlessly now. I wanted to reduce its weight so it would equal the mass of an actual heart. The work gave me much needed solace.

One day, an unfamiliar cloying scent wafted from Dr. Prendergast's private study in the lab. I gagged into my handkerchief. My hacking turned into a coughing fit, and I doubled over. My legs trembled as I used the workbench to prop myself up. When I mustered my strength, I limped over to Dr. Prendergast's door and knocked weakly. I fell forward when she opened the door. The smell of burning flesh joined with the sickly sweet mystery scent overpowering my senses.

I hacked into my handkerchief.

"May I help you? I'm in the middle of an experiment." A black leather mask covering Dr. Prendergast's mouth and nose muffled her voice.

"I can't breathe. What's that smell?" I wheezed.

"Oh, it must be the formaldehyde." She waved her hand. "My experiment is nearly complete."

Over her shoulder, I spied her experiment. My eyes widened. She had a dead frog resting on a small platform on her desk, along with a generator. Its corpse was being shocked repeatedly, causing it to twitch and flop in place.

"You're duplicating Galvani's experiment? Why?"

Dr. Prendergast tsked. "No, I'm improving it. Look."

With growing dread, I stepped into her study. The poor frog's darkened veins were visible through its translucent skin. She had prepared a makeshift blood transfusion with clear, narrow hoses going between the corpse and a vial of black-red fluid. An arcane symbol in front of a red tear-shaped blood-drop was etched into the vial.

"What is this?" My body was weakening. I could barely stand, but I couldn't take my eyes off the frog.

"I've done it. I've combined the fields of chemistry with its predecessor, alchemy."

"I don't... understand." My brain was foggy. Nothing felt real.

"Just watch."

The generator shocked the dormant frog. It convulsed, twisting violently. Its skin bubbled and popped as muscles expanded rapidly. The generator short-circuited and sparked before going silent.

For a long moment, nothing happened.

The frog croaked, its voice distorted and warbling.

My heart skipped several beats as I staggered closer.

Its baleful eyes locked with mine.

"Why?" I trembled, cold sweat beading across my forehead.

"You said it yourself: we need to test if the lungs and heart will work on a cadaver." Dr. Prendergast pointed at the frog. "It's crude, but it's progress."

"You." I had to stop to catch my breath. It was becoming more labored by the second. My heart palpitated. "You told me we didn't have money to buy a cadaver."

"And that is still true."

I turned around, trying with all my willpower to not collapse.

Dr. Prendergast's clinical gaze was on me. "I'm astounded you've lasted as long as you have. By rights, you should have been dead by now. I don't think it'll be much longer, though. You're looking awfully pale."

Rage and sorrow burned in my failing heart. "Why? I did everything I could to help you!"

I could feel my heart spasming, fighting to keep pumping. It felt ready to burst.

"Not everything, girl. You showed so much promise. Ah, well. You'll still aid my research, even if it's not the way I intended."

I lurched forward, fist raised. I took two steps before I stumbled and fell.

Dr. Prendergast caught me. She slowly lowered me to the floor, kneeling as she held my head in her lap.

Sobs wracked my body. "Not like this." I could barely speak.

"It'll be over soon." Dr. Prendergast stroked my hair, tucking it behind my ear.

A distant part of my consciousness wondered at the gesture.

I closed my eyes.

Everything stopped.

I woke up with a scream ripping from my throat. The scent of formaldehyde invaded my senses. Scorching pain everywhere. Well, not everywhere. I couldn't feel my arms or legs. Dr. Prendergast's curious visage came into view. She was speaking, but I couldn't hear. The words were muffled.

I thought she said, "You're alive?"

The edges of my vision blurred. Soon, the unbearable, burning pain spiked, and the blackness took me.

Again, I woke up screaming. It felt like every nerve ending was on fire. Pain wracked my body. I convulsed, thrashing against the leather straps crisscrossing my torso. My head hit the stiff cushion on the metal table. My throat was raw. Bile churned in my stomach.

Dr. Prendergast's signature bun was in disarray when she appeared in my field of vision. She was holding a flask with arcane symbols etched into the glass. The fluid was black, the consistency of sludge.

"Drink this." I saw the doctor's lips move, but her voice sounded far away. She tipped the bottle into my mouth.

It tasted of sulfur and death. I gagged, then spat the potion all over Dr. Prendergast's pristine lab coat before passing out.

I didn't know who I was, or the name of my tormentor. All I knew was the lab, my restraints, and the foul woman forcing sludge down my throat.

The woman behind my torture was always the same.

Time lost all meaning. I could have been here for days, weeks, or years. For all I knew, an eternity passed.

I don't know how many times I woke up in the lab. Every time, there was pain, screaming, and the smell of formaldehyde. The scene in the lab sometimes varied. I'd see a fresh, viscous chemical solution brewing and additional notes written on the chalkboard.

The woman was always present. Sometimes, she'd be near, forcing me to drink another vile potion. Other times, she'd be sitting on a stool, jotting down notes. Her appearance was increasingly unkempt. Her once pristine white lab coat faded to a dirty gray. The only solace I had was spitting out the elixir on her every chance I could before oblivion took me again.

I woke up in an unfamiliar lab alone. It was painted stark white and furnished with three long worktables, a stool, and a writing desk. A medical skeleton stood at attention in the corner, its lifeless eye sockets staring at me. By the gaslight, I could have sworn it was smiling at me.

Chemical solutions bubbled and fizzed. Blackish-red liquid flowed through a complex series of beakers, flasks, and tubing. At the end of the complicated setup, the syrupy liquid dripped into a labeled vial with an alchemy symbol in front of a tear-shaped drop of blood. The sight of it made me shiver.

Footsteps echoing off the stone floor drew my attention. The woman in white approached. Her thin, silver spectacles were barely visible on her hooked nose. She carried a syringe with a huge needle. I thrashed against my restraints.

"There's no need for that." Her voice was bitter, matching her steely gaze as she sat on a stool next to my table. "I've come to mark your progress." She brandished the syringe. "This is if you don't comply. Are you feeling civil enough to answer my questions?"

When I moved my atrophied muscles, my face ached. I gritted my teeth. "I won't discuss civility while you have me bound."

"That is for your safety as much as it is for mine."

"I highly doubt it."

Silence stretched between us.

She opened a journal and poised her pen, ready to write.

"How are you feeling?"

I let out a barking laugh. My throat ached from the effort.

"You must be joking."

Her nostrils flared, and she gripped her pen so tightly I thought it would break in half. "I can't get data if you don't cooperate."

"Not my problem." I nodded at the restraints strapped across my torso. "I'm held against my will. You've replaced my arms and legs with machines. I know nothing but pain and nightmares." Meeting her gaze, I added, "I don't even know your name."

The woman pushed up her spectacles. "I'm Doctor Prendergast, your creator. I brought you back to life again using my inventions."

I snorted. "Sounds like a half-truth to me."

Dr. Prendergast glared, but didn't elaborate.

Seconds ticked by.

"I don't know my name or what day it is."

"Fascinating. Are you sure? No memory at all?" Dr. Prendergast's lips pursed.

I squeezed my eyes shut. A vision of a daisy on a sweltering summer day floated in my memory. A feeling of warmth came over me, and a single word came to mind.

"Lucille?" I whispered. I opened my eyes.

"Yes." Dr. Prendergast scribbled a note in her journal. "That's your name."

Learning how to walk again was an excruciating experience. Dr. Prendergast had no patience. When I complained about how cumbersome my long, mechanical legs were, she snapped at me.

"Well, if I would have had proper help, I would have had an easier time manufacturing the limbs, wouldn't I?" She cursed under her breath as she picked up the vials that my shaking steps knocked over. "At least your lungs and heart are the correct size," the doctor muttered.

"You should have left me dead. My joints ache." One compressor on my arm hissed as I stretched. The effect was unnerving. Worse was seeing the clear hydraulic tubing attached to my limbs carrying black-red, viscous fluid. If I stared too long at the artificial veins, my stomach churned.

Dr. Prendergast insisted my clothing did not cover any of the new mechanical parts. She claimed it helped her see any mechanical failures. I felt like the humiliation was another form of control. The crudely stitched sackcloth garment made my back itch horribly and left me feeling exposed. She finally relented and permitted me to wear shortened trousers with the tunic, but it was the only concession she would make.

Recovering from my efforts took time. My mechanical lungs were perfectly functional but would leave me in breathless stitches after exerting myself too much. I swear I could feel the machinery at work, but Dr. Prendergast insisted it was my imagination after writing another note.

In my dreams, I could hear my artificial heart pumping like an engine. Steam billowed out of my mouth as it grew hotter and hotter. I would wake drenched in sweat, putting a hand over my pounding heart. It was unnerving, not being able to feel with my hands. I could no longer tell the temperature of things or its texture. I only could feel it was there.

I still didn't understand how I could control my prosthetics.

When I asked Dr. Prendergast about it, she was even more tight-lipped than usual.

"Electromagnetic telekinesis induced by alchemy," she told me brusquely. She refused to tell me more. "It's proprietary, and you wouldn't understand."

Stealing furtive glances at her journal proved to be fruitless. The paranoid doctor wrote in a gibberish code of letters, numbers, and arcane symbols.

Eventually, I figured out it must have been some property of the mechanical limbs combined with the solution she used for my blood. I tried to manipulate the metal buckles on my restraints with my mind, but failed.

Each night, Dr. Prendergast gave me a shot that rendered me unconscious when she was done experimenting for the day, leaving me little time to make my escape attempts.

The day I finally walked across the lab without stumbling, Dr. Prendergast smiled.

"Excellent. You're mastered movement in time for me to present you at the World's Fair."

I didn't know what the World's Fair was, but the grim look in her eyes sent a shiver down my spine.

I woke up in a coffin. I fought the urge to panic, terrified I would run out of air. There wasn't much room to maneuver, but I could lift my hand to feel the lid of my prison. The tips of my mechanical fingers caught on pinprick holes on its surface. I waited for my heart rate to return to normal while formulating a plan. Though I was trapped, at least I wasn't bound again.

I hammered and railed against the insulated lid, to no avail. Feeling brave, I shouted for help until my voice was hoarse, but a leather gag muffled my mouth. It came up to the bridge of my nose, with only narrow slits to allow me to breathe.

I thought I heard voices, but inside the cocooned box, I couldn't know for certain. In the distance, I heard the rumblings of a train and loud crackling.

Drenched with sweat, I pushed with all my strength. My mechanical limbs groaned, twisted, and cracked, but finally, the lid gave way. With a clatter, the lid burst open and the chains confining me snapped under the strain. My arms were mangled, but I was free. Grunting, I lifted myself out of the coffin, trying to not damage my prosthetics any further.

I was alone in the room. Rather, a luggage car. Steamer trunks and lab equipment surrounded me. A machine on the other side of the room was the source of the humming and crackling noise. I shrank away from its hot-white light, shielding my eyes. After several moments of this, I realized it wouldn't do anything to me. I slowly lowered my guard but opted to try the door farthest away from the great machine.

Rain and wind battered me outside the baggage car. I held my arms close, fearful the wind would take what was left of my limbs. It was agonizing opening the door to the next car, but with a groaning heave, it gave way. Despite my injuries, I pulled the door hard enough to dent its edge. I slowly closed it, hoping no one would hear me.

I didn't have to worry. The car I was in was empty. I crept through the kitchen and dining area without incident. The entrance to the next car was enclosed, so I didn't get pelted with rain again when I opened the door. The cushions of the damask-patterned chairs looked soft and inviting to my haggard body, though I didn't dare rest.

The ornamental rug bunched under my heavy boots as I headed towards the next car. I stumbled into the passenger car, bumping into something solid.

I looked down to see a petite, elderly woman peering up at me, squinting up at me through her thick spectacles in the low gas-lamp light.

"Oh, excuse me. I was trying to find the water closet." She smiled, taking her spectacles off to clean them with an embroidered handkerchief. "My goodness, but you are tall. Please forgive me. I need new spectacles badly. These don't work at all, especially in low light."

Afraid to move, I grunted an assenting noise.

"Oh, dear, I didn't mean to embarrass you. Have a pleasant night!" She turned and went down the aisle between the sleeper cars.

I stared after her, stupefied, but finally forced myself to keep walking in the same direction as the stranger. Slowing my pace, I hoped to put enough distance between us and avoid being seen again. I couldn't afford to backtrack. I needed to find somewhere to either carefully exit the train or hide until it stopped. Near the end of the aisle, I encountered the small woman again. This time, she wasn't alone.

Dr. Prendergast was talking to the woman, whose back was turned to me. The doctor's eyes widened when they met mine.

The other woman turned towards me.

Before I could move or warn the passenger, Dr. Prendergast reached into her pocket and shot the tiny woman full of the same syringe she normally used on me.

The woman never registered what happened to her. She instantly collapsed to the floor.

An ugly scowl crossed Dr. Prendergast's face.

"You did this," she told me, then stuck the syringe into my stomach.

Blackness overtook me again as I succumbed to the familiar knockout drug.

The dosage must have been too weak. I regained consciousness in the observation car, my back throbbing as the doctor dragged me along the floor.

My mind was sluggish, but I hooked my arm on one of the chair legs, forcing Dr. Prendergast to release me.

She stared down at me.

I slowly pushed myself up.

"I don't know what you think you're doing, but you'd better go back into storage before anyone else has to die."

I froze.

Dr. Prendergast's eyes were wild. "I had to get rid of the witness. Luckily, she was old enough people will think she accidentally fell off the train. I can't afford to have anyone tip my hand."

With a muffled wail, I fled the car.

When I turned back, I was almost at the end of the train. I contemplated throwing myself overboard after Dr. Prendergast's words, but I wasn't sure if the impact would be fatal in my undead state. I was afraid of irreparably damaging my limbs, surviving the impact, and slowly wasting away.

As I stalked through the passenger cars, I scanned each of the sleeper cars. Most of them had their curtains drawn. I thought about knocking on the door to one to ask for help, but decided against it. I tried a few times to take off the muzzle, but my mashed fingers didn't have the dexterity.

Near the end of the front passenger car, I peered into the dimly lit aisle, looking to see if my presence had disturbed any passengers. I wondered if Dr. Prendergast was following me. The darker part of me wished she were. My cursed blood cried for vengeance.

The door behind me opened with a loud squeak. I whirled around to see a young woman shakily wielding a butcher knife, biting her lip. Terrified she'd wake the passengers, I ran towards the woman. My footsteps thundered down the aisle, my compressors working overtime and hissing.

The noise woke up the slumbering passengers. They stood at the entryways to their sleeper cars and started shouting. When I reached the woman, I tried to put my hand on her shoulder to reassure her I meant no harm.

Her back hit the corner of the doorframe, and she screamed.

She slashed at my hoses with the knife.

She missed, but I stumbled backwards, losing my footing.

There was a sharp pain in my back that was all too familiar.

As the world faded to black, I heard Dr. Prendergast say, "I told you to sleep on the train."

I woke up in the baggage car, bound. A dapper man wearing a crisp, buttoned uniform stood guard over Dr. Prendergast. Neither of them noticed me waking up. I assumed from his hat and uniform he was the conductor. He clutched a six-shooter in his trembling right hand.

Dr. Prendergast looked bored sitting with her hands in her lap, staring at the electrical machine shooting off sparks on the other end of the car.

Seeing the doctor disaffected after what she did to the passenger broke me. I stood, ripping apart the pitiful binding on my wrists. I lumbered towards Dr. Prendergast.

The conductor found his courage. He bolted upright and shook as he fired off six shots in rapid succession at me. He missed. With one sweep of my massive arm, I knocked him out of my path.

Unfortunately, even in my damaged state, my strength was too much. He slumped against the wall, unconscious. At least, I hoped he was only unconscious. I wanted to check, but Dr. Prendergast was inching away from me. When we locked eyes, she scrambled behind a massive stack of luggage and barricaded herself.

I couldn't grasp the tightly wedged steamer trunks to move them out of my way. Briefly, I contemplated pushing the baggage onto the doctor and crushing her, but it didn't feel right. I needed to confront her face to face.

I barely registered the baggage car door opening.

The young woman from the observation car stepped into the car, wielding a shovel. Coaldust clung to her from head-to-toe. She must be the train's fireman. I didn't pay her more attention, as I focused on pushing the luggage out of my way. One of my hands flopped uselessly, hanging on by a hose.

I should have kept one eye on the fireman.

She hopped the barrier to the cargo side and charged. With a single strike from her shovel, she sliced a key hose near my knee. I let out a muffled scream. My injured leg crumpled. Wincing, I turned to face my attacker.

Red tinged my vision. I raised an arm.

The fireman shielded herself with the shovel and squeezed her eyes shut.

I used the frayed ends of my broken mechanical arm to cut the leather muzzle off. I stretched my mouth, grimacing.

The fireman opened her eyes and stared with her mouth agape.

"Finally." My raw throat burned. "Girl, stop hitting me with your shovel. I bear you no ill will. My ire is for my creator, not you."

"No!" Dr. Prendergast shouted. Angry red splotches appeared on her cheeks.

"What about poor Mrs. Olaughlin?" the fireman's voice cracked.

"Who?"

"The missing passenger."

"You mean the poor soul my so-called master pushed overboard when she discovered my escape?" I seethed.

"Let me deal with Dr. Prendergast. She has more blood on her hands than you know."

"What?" The fireman stepped back.

"Everything I did was to protect you! If you had been discovered before the fair, they would have had you destroyed! This is all your fault. You shouldn't have tried to escape!" Dr. Prendergast pointed a bony finger at me.

"I did her no harm. I was escaping you. You drugged and killed that poor woman. My conscience is clear. Your soul, however, is forever tainted. You must face justice."

"Never!"

"You cannot escape!" I knocked the stack of trunks over. My arm hemorrhaged, staining my tunic. I towered over Dr. Prendergast.

"Get away from me, foul, useless creature! You could have been perfect. Now look at you. You're broken. No one will fix you." Dr. Prendergast sneered.

"I was your assistant. How could you do this to me?" All my grief bubbled to the surface.

"I needed a fresh body, and you wouldn't help me get one. The problem solved itself."

The young woman's face blanched. "You would have done the same to me!"

As if noticing her for the first time, the doctor's eyes widened. "Of course, I wouldn't have. You could have helped me perfect her."

I roared and put Dr. Prendergast into a chokehold. The doctor's face turned purple.

"Wait!" the woman lightly touched my arm.

"Why? She doesn't deserve mercy."

"No, she doesn't. You don't want blood on your hands, do you?"

I relaxed my hold on the doctor. "I do not."

"You once had a name, right?"

"Lucille." I frowned. Jumbled memories came back. It

was like watching someone else's thoughts. "I cannot remember my surname, only fragments of my past. Nuns raised me in an orphanage. The doctor took me in. She promised me a better life in exchange for my help. When she was unsatisfied with my work, she murdered me for her experiments."

"Let Dr. Prendergast face justice the right way."

"Very well. I shall submit myself to justice, too." I let go of the panting doctor. My arms were losing black fluid rapidly now. "If I don't bleed out first."

"I can probably fix that," the woman offered. She stepped forward, but Dr. Prendergast was faster. The doctor lunged forward with a syringe.

"You'll do no such thing!" Dr. Prendergast's syringe pierced my skin.

"No!" The woman swung her shovel at the doctor's head. Dr. Prendergast crumpled to the floor. She removed the syringe from my torso. "What'd she give you?" she asked.

"Knockout drug," I yawned, then passed out.

I woke to the young woman hissing in my ear, "Wake up!"

I slowly cracked my eyes open. When I could focus again, I cautiously asked, "Why are you helping me?"

"You deserve better." She offered me a hand to help me up. "Can you walk?"

I took a few shaky steps. "I believe so."

"Good. There isn't much time. I'll help you if you'd like. I have a plan, but I need you to hide."

I stared at the fireman, then at Dr. Prendergast, still unconscious on the floor. "What must I do?"

The fireman told me her name was Rosie, right before informing me her plan was to wrap me in a tarp and bury me in coal. It hadn't occurred to me to inquire about her name when she had asked me for mine. I wondered if my humanity was slipping away. Even more pressing, I wondered if she would leave me buried in the tender.

Rosie only put a light layer of coal on top of the tarp, but it covered my entire body. She had cut a hole in it for a hollow metal tube for my mouth. She assured me she would make sure I could breathe. I hated this plan more by the second, but we were short on time. The last thing I saw before she covered my face with the tarp was her worried expression.

The locomotive started moving again. During the fight in the baggage car, I didn't realize we had come to a stop on the track. The noise of the train thundering down the track was deafening. At least the rain had stopped before Rosie hatched her plan.

Slowly, the train came to a stop. I heard the noise of the passengers leaving and the busyness of the station as cargo was loaded and unloaded. Frequent whistles and shouts of "All aboard!" grated at my raw nerves as I struggled to find a comfortable position.

Hours passed. Breathing through the metal straw was excruciating. I longed to spit the tube out of my dry mouth. Even through the thick tarp, the coal pressed into me and dug into my sides.

Crickets sounded in the distance.

I contemplated pushing my way out of the tender. Surely, Rosie would have come for me by now if she meant to keep her word.

Sudden movement startled me. The weight of the coal was lightening. I heard Rosie's muffled voice.

"Hang on, I'm coming for you!"

I blinked several times when she pulled the tarp off my face. I spat out the metal tube.

"Never again," I wheezed, letting out a hacking cough.

"I'm so sorry. It was the only place I could think of no one would check. Are you okay?"

I flexed my mechanical limbs. Her impressive handiwork gave me more mobility than I had hoped for. "I'm fine. What's next?"

Rosie grinned. "I'm going to smuggle you into the World's Fair. With all these inventors gathering in the same city, someone is bound to have the parts we need to fix you up."

"Thank you. It's good to have a friend."

Rosie helped me climb out of the tender. Evading the night watchman, we snuck out of the station and disappeared into the night. Another downpour started as we neared safety, but it didn't bother me. As it washed away the grime and coal dust, I hoped my past was cleansed, too.

THE RESURRECTION
EXPERIMENT

It has been nearly four months since Rosie and Lucille helped Dr. Evelyn Mendel and the Living Metal Man escape the clutches of Edison's men. Finding themselves unexpectedly furloughed as tensions mount over labor disputes at the railroad company, our heroines return to the World's Fair. The International Electrical Congress is in session, and Rosie hopes to see Nikola Tesla at his demonstration. Unfortunately, outside forces are closing in, threatening to separate Lucille and Rosie forever.

Nikola Tesla's personal exhibit in the Electrical Building was everything Rosie hoped for and more. She couldn't take her eyes off the rotating copper egg, balanced upright, suspended in a magnetic field produced by the magnet coils hidden beneath the polished wooden platform. On the edges of the circular platform, three copper balls orbited around the spinning egg. An elegant placard stated the device was Tesla's Egg of Columbus.

On the wall behind the display hung a poster of the

man himself. Nikola Tesla sat inside a metal Faraday cage, smiling serenely as dramatic sparking arcs of electricity struck the cage. In bold letters, the poster announced a one-in-a-lifetime demonstration on August 25th. Rosie beamed when she realized they'd still be in town for it.

"It looks like the solar system is performing a ballet, doesn't it?" Lucille remarked quietly next to Rosie.

Rosie's eyes shone. "I've never seen two-phase magnet coils used like this before." She retrieved her logbook from her knapsack. Before she could start sketching the device, Lucille winced and stretched. Her pen hovered over the page as Rosie asked, "What's wrong? Do I need to readjust your pivot joints again?"

Lucille smiled ruefully as she rubbed her mechanical arms, concealed by a navy blazer. "No, your repairs last night were perfect. I'm still sore from pulling the emergency brake yesterday." She shook her head. "I think I'm going to stretch my legs and see if the next room is cooler. I'm regretting our decision to dress up. It's too muggy for this jacket. Do you think anyone would be scandalized if I took it off?"

"I don't think anyone would mind, and if they do, it's their problem." Rosie shrugged. Her head-to-toe vitiligo and Lucille's towering height already drew enough stares when they were out. Both of them learned long ago not to mind the attention. A fashion faux pas would be nothing. "Besides, at least this room is empty. I hope you feel better soon."

"Thank you. I'll see you later." Lucille hesitated, then asked, "Do you think we have enough for dinner on the fairgrounds tonight? I'd love to see everything lit up. They say the view is spectacular."

"Let me check." Rosie marked her current page and flipped to the finance section of her logbook, bookmarked by a stack of neat receipts.

The recent labor troubles at the railway forced her to track every penny spent. They both knew coming back to the World's Fair was an extravagant expense, but in a surprise turn of events, their boss, Honora, gifted them with enough funds to cover their unplanned furlough. When Rosie confronted her about the generous gesture, Honora dodged her questions. The veteran engineer made Rosie promise to go enjoy the fair and let her know if she got to see Nikola Tesla's demonstration.

The encounter left Rosie feeling both touched and worried about the future.

After reading through the rows of figures, Rosie closed her logbook. "If we eat sandwiches the rest of the week, I think we can make it work. Honora said she thinks our line will resume soon."

If not, Rosie thought, *we're in trouble*. Despite the knots in her stomach, she forced herself to smile. Lucille almost never asks for anything for herself. She could do this for her.

"So, dinner's on?" Lucille brightened considerably. After Rosie nodded, she slung her blazer over her burgundy shirt and departed for the next room.

Rosie noted with satisfaction the hydraulic system in Lucille's limbs was much quieter after the last few rounds of adjustments they worked on together between shifts. They could both breathe a little easier in public, but they still took precautions, keeping their distance from others.

Alone in the main exhibition room, Rosie's eyes widened as she took in the alternating current motor, rotary transformer, constant potential alternator, and other machines neatly displayed in rows on full tables around the room. Visitors could get close to the unplugged models, so she happily paused often to sketch or make notes in her logbook as she worked around the display tables.

Eventually, Rosie returned to marvel at Tesla's Egg of

Columbus. She devoted a two-page layout to it in her logbook, carefully noting the precise details of the display's set up. The late August humidity was getting to her, too. She thought about stuffing her blazer in her bag as she sketched. She startled when Lucille's voice was directly behind her.

"There's a beautiful lighting experiment set up in the annexed room," Lucille said, causing Rosie to jump.

A quick glance down and Rosie sighed with relief. Her sketch wasn't ruined.

"Sorry." Lucille scratched the back of her neck. "Would you like to see it?"

"I'd love to!" Rosie tucked her logbook under her arm and followed Lucille into the next room.

Inside, a large disruptive discharge coil sat on a table, surrounded by glass Leyden jars. It was stouter and significantly more compact than the Tesla coil that powered the lights on the passenger train they worked on. The coil hummed as it powered lights arranged on an arched copper tube across the room. Hanging on the walls were more lights and phosphorous tubes spelling out names such as Helmholtz, Faraday, Maxwell, and a few names Rosie didn't recognize. She made a note in her logbook to research the unfamiliar names later.

Other tubes on the walls spelled out phrases such as "Welcome, Electricians" in warm, glowing letters. She wondered how Lucille would feel about adding tubes with phrases as part of their apartment's decor and promptly wrote the idea down while Lucille studied the archway of lights.

Rosie was in the midst of sketching the coil when stiff footsteps approached. She looked up to see a wispy woman dressed in a loose, black coat over charcoal breeches standing in the entryway. A black felt hat and spectacles with blue-tinted lenses obscured her expression as she scanned the room.

Something about the woman's stilted mannerisms bothered Rosie enough that she had a hard time focusing on her sketch when she returned to it. Lucille frowned, watching the newcomer from her position by the archway.

The stranger brushed past Rosie, causing her pen to streak across the page.

"Hey, watch where you're- oof!" The stranger shoved Rosie, knocking her to the hard wooden floor.

The woman was unfazed, ignoring everything else in the room except for the disruptive discharge coil. She stalked toward the display, her tall boots tapping softly against the wooden floor.

"What are you doing?" Lucille demanded as she approached the stranger, her heavy footsteps echoing in the room. Her yellow eyes narrowed as she glared.

The interloper ignored both of them and studied the coil, crouching down to examine its power cord. When she stood again, she was motionless and contemplative.

Rosie picked herself off the floor and checked her logbook for further damage while keeping one eye on the rude woman. She harrumphed when she noticed a crease in her page besides the ink slashed across the sketch. She opened her mouth to give the stranger a piece of her mind when she saw Lucille was already behind her.

Lucille clasped the woman's shoulder. "You hurt my companion."

With an unnatural speed, the woman grabbed Lucille's hand and wrenched it away from her shoulder. She dropped low and, with a sweeping kick, knocked Lucille's legs out from underneath her. Lucille fell with a heavy thud. The woman's spectacles clattered on the floor.

Rosie rushed over to help Lucille up and shout at the assailant.

The woman appeared to be uninterested in continuing the fight. She went back to staring at the coil's power cord, immune to her cracked spectacles still on the floor and the obscenities Rosie hurled at her.

Lucille waved off Rosie as she found her footing. She then charged at the assailant, decking the side of her face. Instead of crumpling, as most people would do when hit by a prosthetic fist entirely made of exotic metals, the thief's face slid off and landed on the floor of the exhibition room.

Nonplussed, both Rosie and Lucille stared at the fleshy three-quarters of a face laying on the floor. The three-dimensional nose was the most solid part of it. The rest looked like a crumpled masquerade mask made of the same material as the artificial skin Lucille received from Evelyn to cover her mechanical limbs.

Rosie looked up at the stranger's face. She was immediately drawn to her eyes; they burned like coal. Her nose was a pitch-black hole. The woman's dark tresses were knocked back, revealing simultaneously she wore a wig and the reason for the artificial skin. Where there should have been skin, muscles, and bone, there were mechanical plates, not unlike the automaton Adam's mechanical facial muscles. Steam hissed from the thief's mouth before she clamped it shut. Droplets of sweat clung to her upper lip. Or was it condensation?

The woman and Rosie stared each other down, until the stranger pivoted and effortlessly threw Lucille into the copper arch of lights, shattering bulbs. The arch crashed, taking Lucille with it.

"Lucille!" Rosie dashed to her side.

Lucille untangled her limbs from the fallen copper arch, sending a murderous glare at her attacker.

The assailant leaned over the disruptive discharge coil to unplug it, plunging the room into almost total darkness, save one lone overhead lightbulb. In the dim light, Rosie saw the thief lift the bulky coil, despite her small stature. The Leyden jars clinked and teetered precariously as she dashed towards the exit.

"What the hell?" Rosie chased the thief. She nearly caught the machine-woman, until the thief spun around and shoved her in the chest with the heavy coil, knocking the wind out of her. She doubled over, gasping for breath.

The thief dashed out of the room.

Rosie staggered back to Lucille to help her up. When they both were on their feet, the thief was long gone.

"What was that thing?" Rosie asked. She winced. She could feel fresh bruises already blooming on her chest and back.

"Looked like something the doctor would make," replied Lucille darkly. "Did you see the steam coming out of her mouth?"

Before Rosie could answer, four Columbian guards stormed the room.

"You two better come with us for questioning," a red-faced man with a mustache much too large for his narrow face ordered, pointing dramatically at them. "The thief charged past some of our best men." He narrowed his eyes at them. "How is it you two are so calm?"

Despite the growing sense of dread in the pit of her stomach, Rosie couldn't help replying, "Well, it's a long story."

Lucille collapsed on the bed with a deep sigh as soon as Rosie opened the door to their hotel room. The Columbian Guards had interrogated them for what seemed like hours after storming Tesla's personal exhibit.

"It's too bad they couldn't have been more thorough preventing the theft to begin with," fumed Rosie as she sat her knapsack next to the writing desk in the room's corner. "What was the point in asking us the same questions so many times?"

Lucille yawned. "I think you might have been too honest about the automaton-woman." She closed her eyes and rested her hands behind her head.

Rosie wrinkled her nose while searching through her bag for her logbook and pen. "You'd think they would have given me the benefit of the doubt after the Living Metal Man was a featured performance at the start of the fair, but no, let's keep asking if I've been drinking." She sighed and sat down at the desk. Flipping her logbook to the first blank page, she sketched the thief's face from memory. She pursed her lips as she remembered the breath-like steam coming out of the woman's mouth and the sheen of sweat on her brow.

Next to the rendering, she wrote a note, "Organic machine? Artificial or real?"

"Do you think we should send a telegram to Evelyn?" Rosie asked as she filled in more details on the machine-woman's portrait. She scrunched her nose as she tried to remember what screws were holding together the thief's exposed skull plates together.

Lucille grumbled, cracking open one yellow eye. "What d'you say? I was almost asleep."

Rosie swiveled her chair to face Lucille. "I'm wondering about the design of the coil thief. Her face made me think of the artificial skin she gifted you. Do you think someone stole Evelyn's work?" She held up her logbook.

Lucille groaned. "You're making me get up after the beating I took?" She propped up on her elbows and winced. "I need a minute."

"Don't get up. I'll bring it to you." Rosie's own stiff muscles protested as she crossed the room. She sat down on the edge of the bed and handed Lucille the logbook. "See what I mean? The facial structure is less elegant than Adam's, but how many people do you know of who can make artificial skin or automatons?"

Lucille frowned as she studied the sketch. "You have a point. It's an awfully strange coincidence. I hate to bother Evelyn, but I'm worried." Grimacing, she added, "I can't believe you put her face in your bag."

Rosie flushed. "I wanted to study it. It's not my fault the guards wouldn't take it as evidence." She gestured with her free hand. "I tried to help." She got up to dig through her knapsack. Triumphantly, she returned to the bed with the artificial skin.

"Must you bring it closer?" Lucille scooted back, curling her lips in disgust.

"I wanted to see if it's the same as yours. The consistency is similar." Rosie held the mask to show Lucille. "Do you mind if I check your arms?"

Lucille squirmed. "You can check, but don't let that touch me."

"Deal." Rosie placed the artificial skin on the desk. When she returned, Lucille had her sleeves rolled up.

"Here you go." Lucille held out her arms.

Rosie surreptitiously checked Lucille's mechanical limbs for injuries as she examined her smooth, artificial skin. Everything seemed in order. No tears in the artificial skin, and all the metal pieces appeared to be in place.

"I know what you're doing," Lucille interrupted. Rosie flushed crimson as she chided her. "I'm fine. If I need repairs, I'll be the first one to let you know. I have no interest in falling to pieces." Smirking, Lucille added, "Did you find anything?"

"I mean, they feel similar, but it's hard to tell." Rosie

shook her head. "You can't blame me for making sure you don't need repairs. Those hits were brutal. Are you sure you're okay?"

"I'm fine, I promise." Lucille stretched. "Maybe you should send the mask to Evelyn. She might know something about it."

"Good idea, though I am definitely going to mention it in the telegram." Despite her unease about the theft and the unknown machine-woman, Rosie couldn't hold in her laughter as she packed the mask back into her bag. "Can you imagine the look on her face if I sent it with no note?"

"You're terrible!" Lucille tried to look sanctimonious but failed miserably as she dissolved into giggles.

"I would never." Rosie sobered as the open logbook on the desk caught her attention. She got up to examine it closer. Looking at the sketch of the machine-woman, a horrible thought crossed her mind. She dropped the artificial skin on the floor. Shooting a frightened look at Lucille, she asked, "Do you think she's Dr. Prendergast's work?" She held up the sketch again.

Lucille shook her head. "I don't know." Her expression grew somber, and she sat up straighter. "If she's the doctor's work, then we need to leave. Now."

Rosie's stomach dropped. "Do you think she knew to look for us? It seems like a long shot, doesn't it?"

"I don't know, but doesn't it seem like too much of a coincidence the theft occurred while we were at the exhibit?" Lucille looked down. "Maybe I'm paranoid. But I can't shake this dreadful feeling."

Rosie closed her logbook with a snap and strode across the room to sit next to Lucille. "Trust your gut. We can go somewhere else. What do you need?"

"Right now? I don't know." Lucille's eyes were brimming with tears as she trembled. "It feels like everything is falling apart." Her arms were folded protectively against her chest.

Rosie nodded. "I'll start packing."

"Thank you." Lucille frowned. "But what about the demonstration?"

Rosie paused shoving clothes into their steamer trunks. "If they catch the thief before the demonstration, we can go. But do you even want to stay in the city?"

"Is there anywhere we'd be safe?"

Urgent knocking cut Rosie's reply short. Both of them jumped, startled by the intrusion. Lucille yelped in pain as she landed wrong against the iron headboard.

They waited with bated breath.

"Telegram for you!" It was the nasally voice of the innkeeper.

Rosie let out a breath. "Maybe it's Honora about the schedule. I'll get it." She got up to answer the door.

"Be careful." Lucille stood, too, twisting her hands anxiously.

"I will." Rosie opened the door a crack, leaving the chain on the door. "May I help you?"

"Finally! I was about to slip it under the door." She grumpily handed over the telegram through the small opening.

"Whose it from?" Rosie asked, accepting the yellow envelope.

"Why don't you read it and find out? I have other guests, you know." The innkeeper huffed and marched back downstairs before Rosie could ask anything else.

Shaking her head, Rosie bolted the door's lock and sat down next to Lucille with the telegram. She ripped open the envelope.

"Is it from Honora?" Lucille's voice was full of trepidation.

Rosie turned over the telegram, read the short missive, and dropped it.

"No. We need to leave."

Lucille picked up the telegram and read it aloud. "Meet me at 7116 Lafayette Ave. at 6 pm tonight. Both of you."

It was signed, "Mother."

It didn't take long for Lucille and Rosie to pack and check out. The disgruntled innkeeper barely bid them a sour farewell before they were out the door, pulling their trunks behind them down the busy street. The station was only a short walk away, for which Rosie was especially grateful for. She didn't want to wait for an omnibus. After reading the telegram, she wanted to put as much space between her and Chicago as possible.

Her heart twinged as she thought of missing Nikola Tesla's demonstration, but she had a feeling Dr. Prendergast would never stop pursuing Lucille.

The last thought made Rosie stop in the middle of the sidewalk, causing her trunk to tip over.

"What is it?" Lucille hissed after apologizing to the disgruntled pedestrian who hit her foot on Rosie's trunk.

Rosie looked wildly around the crowded street before pulling Lucille into the nearby alley. Poor Lucille dragged both trunks behind her as Rosie yanked on her arm.

"What has gotten into you?" Lucille asked once they were in the alley. She wrinkled her nose at the garbage piled high against the brick walls. "Couldn't we talk on the train?"

"No. I don't know." Rosie wrung her hands. She paced in the alley, taking several shaky, deep breaths.

"You're scaring me." Lucille put a hand to Rosie's forehead. "Are you feeling sick?"

"No, it's not that." Rosie ceased her pacing to look at Lucille. "If the doctor knows where we were staying, she might know where we live, too."

"No." Lucille's ashen skin paled. She swept back strands of hair that escaped from her slouchy newsboy cap. "What do we do now?"

Rosie took a deep breath. "You board the train to anywhere but home. I don't think going to Evelyn's would be a good idea, either. Anyway, telegram me when you get somewhere safe, and I'll catch up."

Lucille raised her eyebrows. "You're the one with her address in your logbook. What are you planning? I thought our deal was together or not at all." Her voice grew louder as she talked. Passersby peeked into the alley at them before shrugging and moving on.

"I was hoping you wouldn't ask." Rosie studied the laces of her boots, refusing to meet Lucille's inquisitive gaze. "I'm going to confront the doctor. Alone," she added hastily before Lucille could interject.

Lucille opened and closed her mouth, fuming. She lifted a finger. "Like hell you are! Why would you do such a reckless thing? If the thief is working for the doctor, she'll snap you in half! Remember how easily she threw me?" The color returned to her face, flushed with anger.

"I'm worried the doctor won't stop hunting you. I want to end this once and for all." Rosie stood on her toes to match Lucille's height. Despite her own tall frame, Lucille still towered several inches over her. "Besides, I did well enough against the mad chemist when he went berserk. I'll figure out something."

Lucille shook her head. "You're going to get yourself killed." She let out a defeated sigh. "You are right about one thing, though. I don't think she's ever going to stop."

She set her jaw. "I should be the one to confront her. You get on the train. I've already involved you too much."

"Absolutely not!" Rosie had more to say, but the sound of someone or something dropping in the alley behind her made her freeze. Footsteps padded closer, with the confident rhythm of a predator closing in on its prey.

"Run." Lucille's eyes were wild. She didn't wait for Rosie's legs to move. She half-carried her down the alley. Rosie's knapsack painfully whacked her back repeatedly. She hoped it wouldn't slide down and hit her in the back of the head.

They were nearly free.

"Neither of you are going anywhere." A familiar voice echoed throughout the alley. Dr. Prendergast rounded the corner and walked towards them. Her once brunette hair was now bottle-red, though it kept its lone white streak. Otherwise, she was much the same, wearing her signature white dress and sneering over her half-moon spectacles at them.

Behind the doctor, a horseless carriage blocked the alley's entrance. Steam billowed around it as its motor rumbled.

"I left it running. We need to talk." Dr. Prendergast smirked. "How I've missed you, dear creature."

Rosie covertly peered around Lucille to confirm a suspicion. Her stomach plummeted. The thief from the Electrical Building was directly behind them, staring with her coal eyes. She hadn't replaced her missing false skin. It looked like her face was patchwork, living flesh stretched too thin over a mechanical skull. Steam escaped out of her nose and nostrils as she stood guard.

Rosie took a sharp intake of breath. "Shit."

Lucille held her closer.

Lucille let go of Rosie and threw one of their trunks at Dr. Prendergast with all of her might.

Unfortunately, Dr. Prendergast's minion was impossibly fast. In the blink of an eye, she was there, catching the trunk and tossing it to the side as if it were nothing.

"Run," hissed Rosie. She barely registered Lucille picking her up again as they both rushed past Dr. Prendergast and her creation.

"I don't think so." The doctor shook her head. "Christine, stop them."

The thief yanked Lucille backwards. Rosie fell from Lucille's arms and onto the rough cobblestone. The assailant's burning eyes flashed white-hot when they caught the light, then cooled to dying embers when she stared at Rosie, pinning Lucille with one arm.

A chill went up Rosie's back as she got to her feet. "Let her go. You have a new experiment. You don't need Lucille."

Dr. Prendergast took a few steps into the alley. Behind her, pedestrians cursed the horseless carriage for obstructing the walkway, but the vehicle blocked their view of the alley. Its dark curtains were drawn closed, and it was several feet taller than Lucille. No one would come to their aid.

Rosie stumbled backwards when she realized Dr. Prendergast was right in front of her.

"I will decide whether I need my creation. Don't think I've forgotten your role in this, thief," the doctor snarled. Angry red splotches spread from the apples of her cheeks and down the sides of her neck. The vein on her forehead throbbed. Rosie half expected the doctor to be foaming at the mouth.

Rosie reached for her pocket knife.

"I wouldn't do that." Dr. Prendergast inclined her head to her creation. "Christine?"

Lucille cried out as Christine tightened her grip.

The knife trembled in Rosie's hand as she shook with helpless rage. "What do you want with us?"

"I want reparations, thief." Another shiver went up Rosie's back. "You stole my life's work, just as I was ready to exact revenge on my detractors. You're both going to pay."

"You stole Lucille's life! She owes you nothing!"

"I gave her a new life. Without me, she was nothing." Dr. Prendergast rubbed her temples. "This back and forth is tedious. You two owe me, and I'm here to collect."

Rosie let out a derisive snort. "Good luck with that."

There was a hard glint to Dr. Prendergast's gaze. "Oh, really? Let's say you escape. Where would you go? Back to the cozy hotel on 63rd Street? Or your quaint apartment in Philadelphia? Or would you go hide in upstate New York with that so-called doctor and her machine-man?"

All the air went out of Rosie's lungs.

"I never let either of you out of my sight for long. There's nowhere you can go that I won't find you." Dr. Prendergast was close enough to Rosie that she could feel her breath on her clammy skin. "I only needed to bide my time."

"You monster!" Lucille broke free from Christine's grip with a roar and barreled towards Dr. Prendergast.

"You never learn, do you?" Dr. Prendergast idly waited for Lucille to reach her, then shot a syringe into her torso.

"Lucille!" Rosie rushed to catch her friend. Christine pulled her back. Her metal fingers pinched and dug into Rosie's arms as the machine-woman dragged away her from Lucille.

"I don't even know why I bother sometimes," Dr.

Prendergast sneered. She pulled out a second concealed syringe from inside her dress sleeve and shot Rosie's arm full of the same knockout drug. It burned going in.

Feebly, Rosie dragged herself to Lucille's side.

The last thing Rosie heard before she passed out was Dr. Prendergast ordering Christine to load them up in the steam-powered carriage. "Quickly! We've already attracted too much attention."

The blackness took Rosie as she clutched Lucille's hand.

Rosie woke up in a darkened room to Lucille shaking her awake. A foreign, cloying smell assaulted her senses. Her back throbbed from collapsing on the cobblestone in the alley. Painful scrapes and bruises crisscrossed her entire body.

"Thank goodness. I thought you'd never wake up." Even in the low lighting, Rosie could see where tears had streaked down Lucille's cheeks. Fresh cuts over her scarred visage made Rosie's blood boil.

"I hurt too much to be dead." Rosie groaned as she sat up on the cold metal floor. "Where are we?"

"I don't know where we are exactly, but I have a horrible feeling about the room." Lucille clenched her fist. "From what I can see, she's set up another lab in a townhouse. I woke up as the carriage pulled up to the building. The doctor had her minion put us in a cage."

Rosie began to rise, but Lucille gently tapped her. "Don't stand up. The cage is short. You'll have to crouch. Trust me." She rubbed the top of her head.

Rosie grimaced. "I'll be careful."

Crouching low, Rosie sidestepped to the edge of the

cage. Between the bars, she could see rows of tables, split into two columns, many of them covered with long cloths over lumpy shapes. At the end of the tables, she could see there was equipment set up, but with poor lighting, she couldn't see what its purpose was. She didn't need a closer look to tell her what was under the cloths, though. The room stank of formaldehyde and decay. Sputtering, she covered her mouth with a handkerchief.

"How can you stand the smell?" Rosie hissed at Lucille.

"I can't, but I lost my handkerchief."

"Here." Rosie handed Lucille the spare she always had in her back pocket.

"Thank you." Lucille quickly tied the cloth around her mouth.

A door Rosie hadn't previously noticed across the room opened with a loud creak.

"Good! You're both awake." Dr. Prendergast strode in, with Christine following closely behind her. The doctor pulled a lever on the nearby wall, and the lights flickered on with a dull hum.

Christine stoically waited by the door while the doctor made her way closer to the cage. Rosie noted the doctor's creation had her face back on. It had been smoothed out. A casual observer would never guess what was concealed underneath her skin unless they paid too close attention to her steam breath.

Rosie's eyes widened in panic. Her knapsack was gone! It was nowhere in the tiny cage. She patted her pockets uselessly for her pocket knife, her logbook, anything. Despairing, she turned her attention back to the doctor, who was now only a few feet away.

"Looking for this?" Dr. Prendergast smirked and stepped back. On the table behind her was Rosie's knapsack with all of its contents scattered on the surface.

Her logbook was open on the pages about Lucille's blood. "Your diary makes for fascinating reading."

"It's a logbook," Rosie responded through gritted teeth. "How dare you!"

Dr. Prendergast scoffed. "Coming from you, thief, that means little. But enough. Time's getting away."

"Time for what?" Lucille glowered at her creator from her seated position on the floor of the cage. Somehow, she had arranged her long legs into a cross-legged position. Rosie wondered how she could do so. Her own legs were cramped from the constant ducking and crouching.

"The reason I bothered to bring you here." Dr. Prendergast gave Lucille a dismissive, cursory glance. She turned her attention back to Rosie. "The power source I had Christine retrieve-"

"Steal," Rosie interjected, glaring at the doctor.

Dr. Prendergast cleared her throat and ignored her. "Retrieve from the exhibition is not working with my lab's set up. I recall you had some proficiency with these sorts of things. Your diary seems to support the idea." She looked at Rosie expectantly.

"What on earth makes you think I'd help you?" Rosie scoffed.

"You stole my life's work on the eve of my triumph." Dr. Prendergast's voice was deadly calm. "If you don't fix the power source in a timely fashion, I'll have Christine remove your precious Lucille from the cage and I'll harvest her for spare parts. I will complete my experiment."

Rosie's stomach roiled. "And if I help you, what? You'll let us go? Somehow, I doubt that."

The doctor clicked her tongue. "You'll both be alive. Will you do it?"

"Rosie, you can't," pleaded Lucille. She tugged on Rosie's hand.

Rosie swallowed hard as she met Lucille's gaze. "I don't have a choice. You'd do the same for me."

"Oh, good. I knew you would," gloated Dr. Prendergast. She made a sour face as she looked between the two of them. "I don't understand your unnatural bond with my creature, but whatever." She rolled her eyes before turning back to Christine, who was impassively watching the conversation from the entryway. "Christine! Come help with the cage."

Christine gave a curt nod and walked over briskly to the doctor's side. Her expression was neutral, but when Christine glanced at Lucille, Rosie thought she saw something that looked like curiosity flicker across her face.

Rosie stopped wondering about Dr. Prendergast's creature when she realized the doctor was speaking again.

The doctor pointed a black-gloved finger at Lucille. "You stay back. Thief, come out. Slowly. Christine will snap you in two if you don't comply."

Rosie tried to smile bravely at Lucille as she exited the cage. It was more of a grimace, but it was the best she could do. "I'll be okay," she reassured Lucille, who was shaking. "I'll come back to you."

"You better." Lucille wiped away at the tears forming in the corners of her eyes.

"Enough. Get out," commanded the doctor.

Rosie scrambled out of the cage. Much to her surprise, Christine offered her a hand to lift her up. Briefly wondering if this was a ploy to break her fingers, Rosie hesitated before accepting Christine's hand. She was surprised by how warm it was, even through the black work gloves she wore, similar to the doctor's. Before she could comment on the heat, Christine quickly let her hand go as soon as Rosie was standing.

"Come with me." Dr. Prendergast beckoned towards the electrical system across the room.

With growing trepidation, Rosie followed the doctor to the disruptive discharge coil. Christine's soft footsteps followed close behind.

Rosie didn't know if she wanted to laugh or cry when Dr. Prendergast showed her how she had configured Mr. Tesla's coil.

"Well? Can you fix the power source?" The doctor asked after Rosie finished inspecting the breakers and coil. Her arms were folded, and she looked like she'd rather be anywhere else.

Rosie composed herself and straightened. "First, it's not a simple power source. It's a disruptive discharge coil. It uses a transformer to step up the power." She pointed at the transformer connected to the coil. "This one is operating at a fraction of its potential. This transformer is rated nowhere near what you need it to be to increase the output of the coil. At this rate, it'll only power a few bulbs and a simple motor." She pointed to the damaged Leyden jars. "You also need to replace the cracked Leyden jars and add more to the bank. You'll have a capacitor problem if you don't."

Dr. Prendergast harrumphed. "What needs to be done to make it work? Biomedical engineering is my specialty, not all of this electrical business."

Rosie looked at the circuit breaker. When she silently read off the amperes rating on each one, an idea took hold. It was simple, but risky as hell. And yet... She considered her options. She hoped Lucille would forgive her. With her mind made up, she looked at the doctor. "As much as I detest your work, I believe so. I need to see exactly what it is you're trying to power first."

The doctor gave her a cold, calculating look. "Very well."

Dr. Prendergast led Rosie to one of the cadaver tables, with Christine shadowing behind her. She pulled the cloth off the corpse.

Bile rose in Rosie's throat. She clamped her hand over her mouth and nose. Even while wearing a handkerchief, the smell of formaldehyde was overpowering. The body must have been fermenting in the chemical for days. The corpse's hair had been shaved to accommodate electrodes stuck around the circumference of her head. On the body, the doctor had replaced one arm and leg with mechanical parts.

At the end of the table, Bunsen burners were on low heat underneath the all-too-familiar vials of the black-red chemical that Lucille also had running through her veins. The liquid flowed from the vials through transparent tubes into the body.

"I've seen enough," Rosie finally said, her voice muffled by her hand and handkerchief. "Can you please cover the body back up? I'm going to be sick."

Dr. Prendergast rolled her eyes. "You'd think as much time as you spend with my creature, you'd be fine." She pointed at Christine, who promptly covered the corpse back up.

Rosie walked over to the coil. "Do you have paper and a pen? I'll list the parts needed to make the coil work." Her nerves tingled with anticipation. She was so close. She only needed to hold it together for a little while longer.

The doctor retrieved some writing supplies from another table for Rosie and handed them over eagerly.

Rosie took care to write in a larger, neater script than she used in her logbook. She had to be sure the doctor read the precise ratings.

Dr. Prendergast snatched the paper out of Rosie's

hands as soon as she finished writing. Rosie winced at the paper cut on her left hand and silently glared at the doctor while she read over the list.

The doctor looked up from the paper, doubt clouding her haughty features. "This can't be right. How can the transformer be rated so high for such a small coil?"

Rosie put her hands on her hips. "How many bodies do you have in here?"

"Twenty-four. Why?" Dr. Prendergast narrowed her eyes.

Rosie fought the urge to vomit. Twenty-four souls lost to the madwoman. How many more were lost before these? With all the confidence she could muster, she replied, "Then you need more power. The extra Leyden jars along with the new transformer will make it work. I'm not interested in blowing up myself or Lucille."

"Fine. I'll acquire the parts." Dr. Prendergast pointed at Rosie. "Christine, escort her back into the cage. We have some parts to shop for."

Wordlessly, Christine led Rosie back into the cage where Lucille had waited anxiously, sitting as close to the bars as she could.

After Christine locked the cage, Rosie called out to Dr. Prendergast, "Some of those parts will be scarce, especially the transformer."

Dr. Prendergast scoffed. "It's a big city. I think I'll manage."

After the doctor and Christine left, Rosie waited until their footsteps were out of earshot. She let out a hysterical laugh, much to Lucille's alarm.

"What did you do?" asked Lucille, worry etched into her features.

Rosie shook her head. "If the doctor follows my instructions, the transformer is going to explode."

Lucille's jaw dropped. "Are you crazy? We're still in here. The cage is locked!"

Rosie's expression turned grim. "I know. And I'm sorry. It's the best I can do while she has us trapped." She took a breath. "I also think we have to do everything we can to stop her from raising two dozen cadavers. I'm sorry I couldn't talk to you about it first."

"I understand." Lucille looked downcast. "What are we going to do, though? I've already had a second chance at life. I accept my fate. What about you?" She wrung her hands, causing the metal beneath her artificial skin to clack together.

Rosie smiled softly. "It will be fine. See this cage? I'm willing to bet the doctor knows nothing about Faraday cages. We'll be safe from the voltage in here, as long as we stay inside." Her expression grew serious. "We have to last in here long enough to not let the flames and smoke consume us. Then we pick the lock. I'll smuggle tools in here, somehow."

Lucille nodded resolutely. "So as long as we're in the cage, we'll be fine?"

"Yes." Rosie fought the urge to panic. Her calculations were correct. She only needed Dr. Prendergast to take the bait.

It was a restless night for Rosie and Lucille. The knowledge of the bodies only a few feet away and worries about the doctor discovering Rosie's plan plagued them both. The next day, the exhausted pair were woken up by Dr. Prendergast calling for Lucille to help Christine carry in the new equipment.

By Rosie's count, it was August 23rd. She couldn't help

but think about Nikola Tesla's demonstration scheduled to take place in two days while Lucille helped drag the transformer into the lab with Christine pushing. She wondered if it was still on with the theft of the coil.

Rosie shook her head. This was no time for daydreaming. Soon, Dr. Prendergast was at the cage's door.

"I've acquired the parts and tools you've requested." The doctor unlocked the cage. "Time for you to get to work."

Rosie's back was stiff from sitting and laying in the cage. Aside from a few humiliating trips to the water closet under guard from Christine, she and Lucille had passed the time crammed together. She stretched, wincing at the noises her back and joints made, and inspected the transformer. "Can I have my tools back?" she asked the doctor, eying her knapsack.

The doctor waved her off. "Yes, fine. Just get the coil working." The doctor tidied a loose strand of hair from her severe bun. "I have business to take care of while you work. Christine will make sure you finish in a timely fashion. Understood?" Dr. Prendergast gave Rosie a hard look. "You are wise enough to know I'm a woman of my word."

"Of course," Rosie replied nonchalantly. "I'll get started right away."

The doctor scowled. "You're being too cooperative."

Rosie furrowed her brows. "Why wouldn't I cooperate? I don't want Lucille hurt."

"Very well. See to it that the work is done." With that, Dr. Prendergast left the room, her white dress billowing as she strode out the door.

Lucille and Rosie exchanged an uneasy glance with each other. Christine resumed her post by the door, staring lifelessly. Not for the first time, Rosie wondered if there was anything organic left of her.

"I can take care of the wiring," Rosie whispered. "If you'd hand me the tools, so it looks like we're busy, maybe you can stay out longer."

Lucille nodded, and they got to work.

Rosie hated herself a little for the pride she felt as she worked on connecting the coil to the transformer. She felt guilty knowing what this was going to do to Nikola Tesla's device, but it would be a tragedy to let his invention be an instrumental part of the doctor's ghastly scheme. If she got out of this alive, she'd send him a letter and tell him what happened, she decided as she hooked up another coupling.

Lucille was wonderful in her role as assistant, knowing exactly what Rosie needed almost before she asked for the tool. Rosie was worried about the distracted expression on her face, though. She kept glancing back at the machine-woman.

As Rosie checked over her work, Lucille called out to Christine. "Excuse me, Christine?" To Rosie's horror, Lucille took a few steps closer to where the machine-woman stood guard.

"Lucille! What are you doing?" Rosie almost dropped her cutters.

Christine also seemed taken aback. She retreated closer to the door, shaking her head.

Lucille stopped and gave Christine a puzzled look. "What is it? You'd think as fellow experiments, we'd have more in common. I only wanted to talk." She held up her hands, palms up.

"Then you're a fool," Christine whispered. Her voice was much rougher than her delicate appearance. Rosie had to strain to hear her.

"Why do you say that?" Lucille whispered back. "We

could help you. Rosie helped me escape from the doctor before. We can do it again."

A tense silence followed as Christine stared hard at Lucille. Rosie pretended to keep work while contemplating what she could use to incapacitate the machine-woman if she laid a finger on Lucille.

"I can never escape," Christine finally said. She pointed to the back of her neck. "The doctor, in her infinite wisdom, added a safety feature to my design. To have a more obedient experiment, she included a self-destruct function only she can use. She said it'd keep her rivals from discovering her secrets." Her mouth twisted. "I guess I still want to live because I don't dare defy her. I've seen her destroy her Resurrected for less. She's using recycled parts in this experiment." She pointed to the covered tables.

"Her Resurrected?" Lucille's brows furrowed.

"That's what she calls us." Christine shrugged. "I've never been able to talk to another one before. Usually, they wake up and all hell breaks loose."

"How does the self-destruct device work?" asked Rosie, looking up from her work on the electrical systems. "Maybe I could disable it?"

Christine snorted, sending puffs of steam out of her nose. "I know the doctor spoke highly of you, but I doubt it. She never enlightened me as to the specifics of how it works." Her burning eyes met Rosie's. "For all I know, she's lying, but it's a risk I can't take."

Christine's eyes widened. To Lucille, she said, "Get back in the cage. I've said too much. I was supposed to have you go back as soon as your friend started working. Hurry!"

Lucille scurried back to the cage, glancing over her shoulder one last time at Christine. She went back to standing like a sentry, staring straight ahead at nothing at all.

Rosie fretted as she finished her work. Was this the fate in store for Lucille, too? Covertly, she studied Christine. Somehow, she'd free her. She only needed more time.

Dr. Prendergast's brisk steps coming down the stairs dashed her hopes of rescuing Christine.

"Are the preparations complete?" Dr. Prendergast asked after reentering the lab. She looked rather pleased with herself. Wherever she had gone, she appeared rejuvenated with the color back in her cheeks. "I've given you adequate time to get the circuit working." She tapped her foot.

"Yes, it should work," Rosie replied. She wasn't able to hold back the contempt in her sneer.

The doctor sniffed. "Good. Back in the cage with the beast. I won't have you interfering with my work." She flicked her wrist towards Lucille.

Rosie tried to school her expression into one of calm and innocence as she walked back to Lucille. The plan was working perfectly. She felt guilty about Christine, but there was nothing she could do now. Rosie hoped Christine's supernatural abilities would help her survive, but she worried about all the metal in her body. At least Lucille would be protected by the makeshift Faraday cage.

"Christine, you stand guard by the door. If any of the Resurrected try to escape, you know what to do." Dr. Prendergast was positioned by the breakers now. It was only a matter of time.

Christine bowed slightly and turned on her heel, proceeding back to her post.

Rosie was nearly in the cage. She felt Dr. Prendergast watching her the whole walk back.

As Rosie opened the cage door, held open by Lucille, the doctor interrupted.

"I've changed my mind. You're going to flip the switch. I need to see if your repairs were enough." Dr. Prendergast pointed at Rosie.

Rosie's blood ran cold. She looked at Lucille, swallowed hard, and whispered, "Get to the middle of the cage." Before Lucille could protest, Rosie put a finger to her lips. "Don't give away the plan."

Lucille nodded, tears brimming in her eyes. Instead of whatever she was thinking, she blurted, "You can't help her with this! It's monstrous."

Rosie smiled sadly at Lucille. "I'm sorry."

Rosie marched back to Dr. Prendergast, shoulders squared. "I'm insulted you're questioning my work, but if it gets you to leave Lucille alone, well, I'll play along." Her hand was at the breaker's lever.

Doctor Prendergast rolled her eyes. "Hurry."

It was all too much for Lucille. "This isn't together or not at all!" She stayed in the middle of the cage, as Rosie told her to do, but she couldn't look away.

Rosie gave her a watery smile. "I know."

Dr. Prendergast looked suspiciously at them both. "What are you-"

Rosie pulled the lever.

There was a boom, then a steady hum. The lights flickered. The corpses convulsed as the arc flashes fried the bodies. A massive plume of smoke rose from the transformers as a fluorescent blue fire engulfed the electrical equipment.

Rosie knew it'd take some time for the transformer to step up the power. Now, she'd have a slim chance to get back into the cage. She sprinted, thankful she wouldn't have to pick the lock after all. The doctor's ego was so inflated she had grown lax about locking the cage.

Ozone burned and smoke filling the room made Rosie's eyes water and her throat itch, even with her handkerchief covering her nose and mouth. Running was excruciating.

"You did this!" Dr. Prendergast lunged at Rosie as she almost made it inside the cage.

"Rosie!" Lucille screamed. She tugged on Rosie's arm, trying to pull her in.

Rosie groaned as Dr. Prendergast pulled hard in the other direction. Lucille was stronger, but Rosie felt like she was being torn in half. With a last heave, Lucille won the tug-of-war and pulled Rosie inside the cage. Unfortunately, Dr. Prendergast was still attached to her ankle.

The doctor sneered. Before Dr. Prendergast could finish saying whatever vile thing she was thinking, Christine ripped her out of the cage, off of Rosie's leg.

Rosie scrambled to slam the door shut to complete the Faraday cage as Christine grappled with the doctor.

"Get to the middle!" she shouted at Lucille. They huddled together in the center of the small cage and watched Christine and Dr. Prendergast clash as arcs of electricity shot wildly around the room. Rosie was right. Though the outside of the cage was struck by wayward arcs, they were safe inside.

Dr. Prendergast held Christine at bay with one of her syringes. She advanced, wielding the syringe like a knife.

In a flurry of movement, Christine shoved the doctor into the side of the cage, rattling it. Rosie jumped at the noise.

Dr. Prendergast let out a frightened shriek as she slumped to the floor, dropping the syringe.

"What are you doing?" The doctor gasped.

Christine's sleeves were rolled up. She peeled off the

artificial skin covering her arms like taking off a pair of soiled gloves. Her mechanical limbs flexed menacingly. Electricity crackled off her fingers and forearms as she reached for the doctor cowering on the floor. Her living and artificial flesh were burning, with embers smoldering on her face. Steam rose around her head in a hazy halo.

"Stop it! You belong to me." With renewed courage, Dr. Prendergast pushed herself off the floor and crept closer to the circuit breaker, all the while never taking her eyes off Christine.

"No. We belong dead." Another jolt of electricity hit Christine's arms, sending spasms throughout her body.

Dr. Prendergast took advantage of Christine's seizure and sprinted to the breakers. Her hand was on the lever, ready to pull up.

Christine stopped convulsing long enough to close the gap to Dr. Prendergast. She pinned her creator to the breakers. With her other hand, she wrapped her metal fingers around the doctor's pale throat. The disruptive discharge coil arced again. Electricity surged from Christine's arms, through Dr. Prendergast, and through the breakers.

Sparks flew everywhere.

Equipment sizzled, popped, and exploded.

Dr. Prendergast's screams echoed throughout the lab, drowning out everything, until at last, they finally stopped.

Rosie would never forget the lingering smell of blood mingling with burning flesh and ozone crackling for as long as she lived.

The fire damage was finally too severe for the coil to function anymore. With a brilliant flash, it went up in flames.

"Christine!" Lucille wailed, but the other woman didn't respond. The smoke obscured everything now.

"We need to go," Rosie choked out. It seemed the smoke was affecting her more than Lucille.

Lucille nodded. Using her broad shoulders, she slammed the cage open. She stumbled to Dr. Prendergast and Christine's prone bodies. "Christine's not breathing!" She turned towards Rosie, pleading.

"I'm so sorry." Tears filled Rosie's eyes. She coughed and sputtered, "There's nothing we can do for her now."

As if in response, the walls of the lab gave a great shudder. Debris crashed down. Lucille grasped Rosie's hand. Together, they raced out of the lab, up the stairs, and out of the townhouse to an unfamiliar street. Both took huge gulps of air, hands on their knees, as they caught their breath. Rosie was overcome by exhaustion, swaying on the spot. The weight of her knapsack was too much. Lucille caught her before she collapsed.

Outside, the sky was glowing electric blue-green while the building burned white-hot. A humming noise droned in Rosie's ears. Lucille had her slung over her shoulder as she ran through the adjacent alley between it and the next townhouse. Neighbors stood on the sidewalk, gawking at the inferno and the clouds changing colors from blue to green and back again in a hypnotic, pulsing rhythm above the block. No one paid any mind to the two women with singed clothing limping across the street.

When they reached the other side of the street, Rosie struggled to stand on her own.

"What are you doing?" Lucille hissed, monitoring the growing number of witnesses standing on stoops in their nightclothes.

"I need to be sure she's really gone." Rosie moved behind a majestic oak tree. "Here, is this better?"

Lucille nodded, swallowing hard. "I want to know, too." She positioned herself behind Rosie, peeking over the top of her head. Hesitantly, she added, "I wish we could have saved Christine."

"Me, too."

With bated breath, Rosie watched as a fire engine raced around the block and came to a skidding stop in front of the building. The flames were dying down, but the smoke was thick. She could still smell the burning ozone from the Tesla coil. She wondered if her sense of smell had been permanently damaged. The firefighters dumped bucket after bucket on the townhouse, but the building was a lost cause.

Startled shouts came from the firefighters. A silhouetted figure flung open the front door of the crumbling townhouse.

Rosie tensed, and Lucille clutched her hand.

The figure took a few stumbling steps. The firefighters ran towards the figure, but something stopped them in their tracks. Frightened cries rang out. The figure looked around at the chaotic scene. When the figure turned, Rosie could see Christine's burning eyes staring directly at her and Lucille. She wasn't sure if Christine could really see them or not, but she could feel it in her soul.

A support beam inside the building gave way, breaking the spellbinding stare-down. The roof collapsed with a thundering crash, scattering the firefighters and nosy neighbors. Christine whirled around, her tattered coat swishing. She raced away from the burning rubble, fleeing into the night.

Lucille spoke first. "I wish she would have come with us. We could have helped her."

"I hope she's okay." Rosie grimaced. "The amount of

current she took in should have left her burned to a crisp. What did the doctor make her out of?"

"I don't know, but I'm glad Dr. Prendergast can't hurt us anymore." Lucille shook her head. "I wish I could be happier about her demise, but I still have so many unanswered questions. I wish I could have found her notes about me." She sighed. "Or at least, been able to talk to Christine more. It would have been nice to have someone around like me."

Rosie squeezed her hand. "I'm sorry we couldn't find out more information about your past."

Lucille grew quiet as she studied the dying embers in the ruins of the townhouse. "Maybe it's for the best. Dr. Prendergast implied there were more people like her. I'm glad the research burned with her."

"Agreed." They stood in companionable silence for several minutes, watching the sky slowly return to pitch black. The stars were obscured by clouds and the hazy remains of the fire. Rosie cleared her throat. "Anyway, you still have me to repair you. I'll keep you functioning to the best of my ability as long as you want me to."

Lucille cracked a smile at Rosie's corniness. "You promise?"

"Always."

Late afternoon the next day, Rosie and Lucille exited the Electrical Building. They were both fuming.

"I can't believe the guard laughed at us," Lucille complained. "Why did you even bother with the letter?"

Rosie had written a letter addressed to Mr. Tesla to tell him the fate of his missing disruptive discharge coil. She left out the details of what Dr. Prendergast had been planning to use the device for, only telling him the doctor had stolen it for nefarious purposes and mentioned some other electrical equipment in the lab in case anything else had been stolen. She convinced Lucille to come with her to the Electrical Building to drop off the sealed envelope to a dubious Columbian Guard.

After the guard laughed, he said he would do what he could to get the letter to Mr. Tesla.

Rosie felt foolish. Her cheeks were still tinged pink.

"I only wanted him to know what happened to his device. The headlines today didn't exactly help." Rosie grimaced. "I didn't expect the newspaper to have a sketch of Christine plastered on the front page." She added ruefully, "Although, I suppose it wasn't entirely unexpected after the explosion. Or the sky changing colors."

She didn't dare say aloud how much it bothered her. The paper mentioned the rubble would take weeks to dig out. It'd be that much longer until they knew with certainty the fate of Dr. Prendergast.

Lucille looked wistful. "I hope Christine's okay."

The Electrical Building was now several feet behind them. They paused by a bench and watched fairgoers going about their business without a care in the world.

"Is there anything else you want to see?" Lucille asked, breaking the silence. Worry lines creased her forehead as she studied Rosie.

"I don't know. It feels weird going back to normal routine, doesn't it?"

Lucille nodded. "Whatever normal means, right? Well, we still have a few more days before Honora told us to check in, so what do you want-"

Lucille was interrupted by a well-dressed gentleman racing up to them, annoying pedestrians as he ran across the thoroughfare. He was out of breath and sweat dotted his brow. Somehow, his perfectly coiffed hair stayed intact.

"Excuse me. Pardon me for a moment." He held up a single finger beseechingly. "I'm not as fit as I might be, I'm afraid."

Rosie let out an inhuman squeak of surprise when the stranger straightened. She'd recognize Nikola Tesla anywhere.

He adjusted his collar and smiled a megawatt grin. "That's much better. Forgive my sudden intrusion, but are you by chance the two women who left this intriguing letter with the guard?" He held up the envelope with Rosie's precise handwriting, now open.

Rosie gaped, willing herself to say something, anything at all, to stop feeling so embarrassed and awkward. Why, oh why, did she write the letter?

Lucille coughed into her handkerchief, poorly disguising her amusement at Rosie's antics. "Yes, the letter is from us. Rosie here is the one who wrote it."

"Oh, I'm so glad. I wanted to thank you both. I'm Nikola Tesla," he said, bowing slightly. "My apologies. I didn't quite catch your names?" His calculating eyes were on them.

Rosie wished the ground would swallow her whole.

"I'm Lucille, and this is Rosie. We work for the railway." Lucille ribbed Rosie, then gave her hand a supportive squeeze.

Mr. Tesla's eyebrows rose. "Fascinating! If you don't mind me asking, what is it you do for the railway? From your letter, it sounded as if you have a solid grasp of electrical engineering concepts. Are you an engineer?"

Rosie's face and neck flushed. "No, I'm only a fireman. I'm self-taught."

"There's no shame in being self-taught," he smiled warmly at Rosie. His expression turned sober. "I have questions about the fate of my coil. How exactly did it catch fire?"

Rosie gulped. "As I mentioned in the letter, Dr. Prendergast was behind its theft, and she was going to use it for unethical purposes. Fortunately, she didn't realize the transformer I told her to use with it would create far too much power for her designs. When it was switched on, the system was overwhelmed, faulted, and caught fire. I'm sorry I couldn't save your equipment, but it was life or death."

"Oh, it is no substantial loss. The design is still up here." Mr. Tesla pointed to the side of his head. "And this Dr. Prendergast, are they-"

"She's presumed to have perished in the fire." There was a hard edge to Lucille's voice.

Rosie patted her arm. Lucille relaxed marginally until a puff of steam escaped from her right leg's compressor.

They both winced. Rosie's recent repair work wasn't her best. Exhaustion made her work sloppy last night. Today, she rushed so they could make it to the telegram office as soon as it opened to send a message to Evelyn to ask if any of her work was missing.

"Ah, I see." His intense gaze rested on Lucille's knee joint, where the steam had emitted. He shook his head, as if to clear his thoughts. "Anyway, I would like to personally invite you both to my demonstration tomorrow night. I understand it's in the Agricultural Hall, so there should be plenty of seating, but if you're amiable to my invitation, I'll arrange for you both to be in the VIP section."

Rosie forgot all of her embarrassment momentarily. "We would love to attend!" she gushed, earning a chuckle from the others. She ducked her head.

"Excellent. I'll leave a note with you for the ticket information. If I didn't need to go make final preparations for the lecture tomorrow, I'd be happy to escort you to the ticket booth." He patted his pockets and grimaced. "Do either of you have a paper and pen? I seem to have left mine behind in my haste to catch up."

With trepidation, Rosie handed over her logbook and pen. "You could use a blank page in here."

Mr. Tesla's eyebrows rose as he flipped to a blank page, occasionally looking at Rosie's schematics.

Rosie wondered if it were possible to perish from mortification as he wrote instructions for the ticket taker about the demonstration and signed his name with a flourish.

"These are wonderful," Mr. Tesla said as he handed back Rosie's logbook. He placed a crisp business card in her hand. "This is the address of my New York lab. I'll be returning next week. Should you desire to leave the railway company, I'll have a job waiting for you at my lab."

"Th-thank you." Rosie wondered if she had died in Dr. Prendergast's lab, and this was the afterlife. She could do worse if it were.

Lucille did her best to not laugh at Rosie's dazed expression. "Thank you so much. It was a pleasure to meet you."

Nikola Tesla smiled. "You as well." He bowed again. "Do think on my offer," he added, somewhat anxiously. "I have a revolutionary project underway, and I could use capable help."

Rosie muttered, "We will." She felt like she was floating.

"Take care!" Nikola Tesla walked back briskly to the Electrical Building, no doubt in a hurry to finish preparations for tomorrow's demonstration.

After Rosie and Lucille waved goodbye, Lucille whispered, "Are your feet back down to earth yet?"

Rosie let out a hysterical chuckle. "What the hell just happened? Did Mr. Tesla just offer us jobs?"

"He did. What do you want to do?"

Rosie thought about all those long, backbreaking shifts she worked shoveling coal and times she spent wishing she were somewhere else, bringing the schematics in her logbook to life. "Let's go to the demonstration tomorrow, then we'll go tell Honora goodbye."

"Then apartment hunting in New York?" Lucille smiled.

"Yes." Rosie grinned back at her. "I think we both could use a fresh start."

Dusk fell slowly as Rosie and Lucille meandered towards the Ferris Wheel. The lights flickered on, illuminating the fairgrounds in a warm glow.

"I just remembered that I promised you dinner at the fairgrounds. Still interested?" Rosie asked.

"Finally." Lucille beamed.

ABOUT THE AUTHOR

Kelsey Josephson is a sci-fi fantasy author and member of SFWA and ALLi from the Midwest. She has a deep love for Universal Monster movies, all things related to Nikola Tesla, and iced coffee.

Her work includes Strange Happenings, a gaslamp fantasy series set in an alternate timeline, Forsaken Beauty and the Etherbeast, which was an Ongoing Serial Finalist in the Laterpress 2022 Genre Fiction Contest, and A Tail of Two Worlds, which won multiple awards in the Fictionate.me short story contest.

Find out more at www.kelseyjosephson.com

instagram.com/authorkelseyjosephson

facebook.com/authorkelseyjosephson

tiktok.com/@authorkelseyjosephson

bookbub.com/authors/kelsey-josephson